TRAIL OF FIRE

TRAIL OF FIRE

Julie Coffin

CHIVERS
THORNDIKE

This Large Print book is published by BBC Audiobooks Ltd, Bath, England and by Thorndike Press®, Waterville, Maine, USA.

Published in 2005 in the U.K. by arrangement with the author.

Published in 2005 in the U.S. by arrangement with Julie Coffin.

U.K. Hardcover ISBN 1–4056–3372–7 (Chivers Large Print)
U.S. Softcover ISBN 0–7862–7676–2 (British Favorites)

The text of this Large Print edition is unabridged.
Other aspects of the book may vary from the original edition.

Set in 16 pt. New Times Roman.

Printed in Great Britain on acid-free paper.

British Library Cataloguing in Publication Data available

Library of Congress Cataloging-in-Publication Data

Coffin, Julie.
    Trail of fire / by Julie Coffin.
       p.   cm.
    "Thorndike Press large print British favorites."—T.p. verso.
    ISBN 0–7862–7676–2 (lg. print : sc : alk. paper)
    1. Twins—Fiction. 2. Large type books. I. Title.
    PR6053.O3T73 2005
    823'.914—dc22   2005006292

CHAPTER ONE

'I want you to marry me,' Ryan had said and Anna couldn't believe he had said those words—words she'd perhaps longed for him to stay to her once. But not now . . .

This wasn't the time to be saying them at all, not at his wife's funeral. How would she ever know, now, whether he had killed Laura? Or did I kill her, she asked herself. If only I could remember what happened that day. All I know is hearing the terrible, terrible roar of flames; feeling heat sear my skin; smoke choke into my lungs.

Just like it was that other time . . . and that I can remember only too well.

* * *

Anna was six when she first met the twins, Ryan and Cameron. They were identical, same height, same slim build, their dark hair slightly lightened from sun and sea, with eyes a deep, clear blue.

If you'd asked her, then, which of them she would fall in love with, she couldn't have told you. That came later, much later. Back then, Anna had loved them both.

Every summer, after that, they all spent together. It was a strange sort of relationship.

Anna's grandmother and the boys' grandfather were both widowed and had married each other late in life. Tom Delabole was a potter and supplied several craft shops in the area. Sally, his new wife, painted water colours, and it was at an exhibition in one of the shops in St Ives that they'd met.

So, as their parents worked, the three children came to stay for the long school holiday.

'We hate girls,' Ryan told her at their first meeting. 'You can't share our grandfather. Besides, we've been staying here for years and years. It's our grandfather's house, and now we've got a new grandmother.'

'It's Anna's grandmother, Ryan,' Cameron reminded him.

Anna was soon to discover that Cameron was the peacemaker, always serious, with a rather anxious expression, even as a child.

Ryan smiled. It was the first time Anna had seen his smile, and it was something she was never to forget.

'OK,' he said. 'We'll let you share her then.'

Even as young as she was, Anna realised this didn't seem quite right, but the boys, at ten, were almost grown-up, she decided, and, with Ryan still smiling, she could only gaze back and nod.

It was the beginning of his power over her.

'We're going fishing down on the rocks, Gran,' Cameron said at breakfast the following

2

morning, scraping at the burned edges of a slice of toast.

'And me,' Anna spluttered from the depths of her mug.

'No way!' Ryan growled.

'I'm sure she'll be all right playing on the sand, if you keep an eye on her, boys,' their grandmother, Sally, said, heaping cereal bowls into the deep porcelain sink. 'Don't forget, she's only small and can't swim very well. I'll be down later, with a picnic. Your grandfather's just finishing off some tall vases and he'll need help getting them into the kiln.'

'We don't want to keep an eye on her!' Ryan muttered, his mouth in a straight line.

Ignoring him, Sally pushed a long strand of hair away from her cheek and tucked it under the ribbon that held it in an untidy pony-tail.

'You'll be good, won't you, Anna? No wandering off, or paddling in the sea, until I come down there. I won't be very long.'

Anna shook her head, sending her own dark hair swirling round her shoulders.

She nodded, glancing up through thick lashes at Ryan's frown. Cameron spread marmalade on the remaining bit of unburned toast.

'Don't worry. We'll look after her, Gran,' he said.

Anna saw the expression on Ryan's face as he glared at his brother, but couldn't catch the word he muttered into his ear. She'd listened to the sea whispering over the beach before she went to sleep the night before. A strange sort of sound, she thought. Standing on her bed to look out of the window when the sky grew light, she could just see it through the salt-hazed glass.

Now, she couldn't wait to go closer. Sally piled the last of the crockery on to the draining-board and wiped her damp hands on the sides of her trousers.

'See if you can find her a bucket and spade, Cameron. Probably somewhere in the shed at the top of the garden. I expect you and Ryan had some, didn't you, when you were younger?'

She pushed open the side door from the kitchen.

'I really must go and give your grandfather a hand. He never manages to load that kiln properly and then runs out of space if I don't do it for him. I think your fishing rods are in the shed, too.'

Dry strands of grass flicked Anna's legs as she ran across the overgrown lawn behind the boys, arriving out of breath to find them scrabbling through heaps of dusty things.

'There are the rods!'

Ryan tugged at them, sending a couple of canvas deckchairs crashing to the floor. Cameron grabbed the back of Anna's T-shirt, dragging her out of the way as they fell.

'Watch it, Ryan! You nearly had her over!'

'Shouldn't be here then, should she?' Ryan called out over his shoulder as he ran back down the garden.

'Are you OK?'

Anna nodded, rubbing one knee.

'Look, there's a spade under that table, so the buckets can't be far away. What colour do you want? Red or blue?'

Cameron lifted some faded cushions and reached behind them.

'This red one used to be mine and the blue was Ryan's.'

'Blue,' Anna answered without hesitation, and took it from him.

Neither of them knew then, though, that the shed with its jumble of old garden furniture and other clutter was to have such a horrifying effect in their later lives . . .

Thinking back now, Anna could only remember those summers as being hot and wonderful. They couldn't all have been, she knew, but only good things seem to remain in one's memory—or the very bad, and those she didn't want to remember.

She had dreamed of, and waited for, the six weeks spent every year with the grandparents. It never occurred to her that Ryan and Cameron wouldn't be there, too, or that Sally and Tom Delabole were growing older. Life there, for her, could never change.

That first holiday with them all was so different from anything she'd ever experienced.

Her mother and father ran their own art gallery in London. As she grew up, Anna often wondered if a child was something her parents had intended, or whether they had but, not being a very pretty baby, she didn't appeal to their artistic eyes!

All she did remember was the childminder's house—the dark, narrow corridor leading into a large room; the persistent smell of nappies; the chill of plastic flooring; the other children who snatched and pushed; and her own tears.

School wasn't much better. There was always a rush to eat breakfast; tugging on the car seat-belt; her arm stretched as she raced to the playground gate behind her mother; the noise of shrill voices and pounding feet; the loneliness of waiting when either her mother or father was late to collect her at the end of the day. Slowly, she learned what an intrusion they considered her to be in their already busy lives.

Life with her grandparents and the twins was such a contrast, even when Ryan was horrible to her.

Cameron had gripped her hand tightly as they crossed the lane to the beach that first morning. Once they were on the shingle, he'd released it. If Ryan had seen him, Anna could imagine his reaction.

She could see Ryan, on the far side of the cove as he sat on a rock right over the sea. A float bobbed at the end of his fishing line.

'You stay there,' Cameron told her, indicating a patch of dry sand, and pushing the spade into it.

With her gaze still on Ryan, Anna nodded. She'd built a square castle and up-ended four buckets of pressed sand to make towers. With her teeth clenching her lower lip, she scraped out a moat. Anna looked at the sea. Waves curled up to creep over the sand, then slid away again, dragging tiny stones with a swish of sound.

The boys sat side by side, watching their fishing lines. They'd been there for a long time but Anna hadn't seen any fish. She picked up her bucket and scampered towards the sea. The first bucketful didn't fill the moat, neither did the second. Each time she came back, the water was gone again.

Anna went deeper out to sea, feeling it soak into her shorts, and held out her bucket to catch the next wave. One of the twins was crouched over her castle when she returned. Anna eyed him warily. Was it Ryan or Cameron? He'd hollowed out the top of her castle and was stuffing bits of dry seaweed into it.

'That's my castle,' she protested.

He smiled at her, a long, slow smile, and she knew it was Ryan.

'Castles have beacons, Anna,' he said. 'Do you know what a beacon is? You light it to let all the people know when the enemy is coming. Go and find some bits that'll burn.'

'What sort of bits?'

'Anything. Paper, lolly sticks. Look, there's a plastic beaker. That'll do.'

Obediently, Anna trotted round picking up this and that and brought them back to Ryan.

'Got any paper hankies in your pocket?'

She tugged one out and watched as he tore it into shreds and added them to the growing pile.

'Now,' he said, rattling a box in front of her face, 'here's the matches. Put some of those on. Then I'll let you light it.'

Anna looked at him doubtfully.

'With the matches?'

'Of course, silly. Go on.'

Ryan pushed a few matches into the heap of debris, then handed one to her.

'Don't you know how to light a match?'

She shook her head.

'Like this. Take it. That's it. Get closer. Closer than that, Anna. Now, light that bit of paper.'

Hand shaking as she held the burning match, Anna leaned over the castle, her chin brushing one sand turret.

With a faint crackle, the flame shot up, twisting towards her. Anna jerked her head away, but Ryan's hand was pressed to her back, holding her there. Acrid smoke filled her nostrils. Anna coughed and felt Ryan's fingers tangle into her hair, pushing her face down. Squirming, she tried to pull away. The neck of her T-shirt tightened suddenly, and she fell backwards as the pressure released.

'Stop that, Ryan!'

Through a blur of tears, Anna lay on the sand, watching as the two boys rolled over and over in a whirl of pummelling hands and feet, her castle scattering round them. A fragment of paper glowed for a moment, before it floated up into the air and was gone.

'Are you OK, Anna?'

Anxious blue eyes were gazing down at her. Anna knew it was Cameron. Still sobbing quietly, she nodded. He held out a hand.

'Come on. I'll take you back to the house.'

Sitting on his heels, he dipped his fingers into her bucket of water and gently wiped them across her cheeks. Anna winced as the sea water stung. Ryan came across the sand and stood in front of them.

'Best not tell your gran, Anna. You shouldn't play with matches, should you?' Ryan said.

Anna opened her mouth to protest, but the expression on Ryan's face silenced her.

'You won't tell her, will you, Anna?'

Silently, she shook her head.

Fire seemed to haunt Anna after that day. It was almost as if that first one lit a trail that was to follow her throughout her life. No wonder she had such a fear of it.

And now, when she couldn't remember what happened on the day of Laura's death, it was haunting her again.

Why, she asked herself, why don't I know? Why has my mind blanked out everything? Was Ryan smiling then? Was he even there? Or was it just me, alone with Laura?

'I want you to marry me.'

Ryan's words throbbed through her brain. How could he say such a thing? And especially here, sitting in the church, with Laura's coffin bearing a sheaf of white lilies—lilies that Ryan had insisted were to be the only flowers laid on it . . . his flowers . . . like her wedding bouquet.

Anna studied him across the aisle, tall, straight-backed, hair just as full as when he was a child, emphasised, maybe, by the stark darkness of his suit. For a moment, as if sensing her gaze, he turned his head and smiled.

A quiver ran down Anna's back. In the solemnity of the church, Ryan's blue eyes were caressing her. His gaze slowly moved over her and, finally, reached her eyes. Swiftly, cheeks burning, she looked away from him, but his smile lingered in her mind.

A candle flickered, its long, thin flame twisting. A trail of smoke spiralled towards her. Anna flinched, closing her eyes. She could smell the melting wax. When she opened them again, the flame had steadied, burning straight and clear—like the flames that day when Tom

Delabole died.

She'd been there then. She remembered the questioning, so many questions . . . about the shed . . . about the candles.

And now, she thought, it's all happening again . . .

CHAPTER TWO

Anna had been ten when her parents decided she was old enough to make the journey to her grandparents alone. 'Children need to be independent at an early age,' her father said. 'Too much coddling nowadays. Never have a chance to think for themselves.'

So Anna was put on the train from London, soon after breakfast. She knew Penzance was her destination and that her grandmother would be waiting to collect her there. The ticket inspector on the train had been instructed to keep an eye on her.

She was asleep when the train eventually arrived at Penzance and would have slept for longer! It was only her panic-stricken grandmother, rattling at the carriage door, that woke her.

'Oh, darling!' Sally cried, hugging her. 'You poor, little scrap.'

After that journey, Anna always knew how to cope on her own.

She was fourteen when Tom Delabole, the twins' grandfather, died. That was a summer she would never forget. Every year, until then, had followed the same pattern. The boys were always there when she arrived. Their school, being a private one, ended its term a week before hers. Her arrival that fatal summer, though, was different. It seemed to set the scene for what was about to happen.

Her grandmother wasn't on the platform to meet her. The other passengers filed their way out until only Anna was left, standing there.

Maybe Gran can't find anywhere to park, Anna thought, picking up her case, or she's had a puncture on the way.

'Anna!'

Tom Delabole was hurrying towards her, his pale blue T-shirt and jeans streaked with clay.

'Grandpa!' she shouted, running into his arms. 'I thought everyone had forgotten me!'

'As if we would.' He grinned. 'No, but your grandmother's had a bit of an accident. Threw us a bit. Let's have that case and I'll put it in the boot.'

'What's happened?' Anna asked anxiously.

Tom climbed into the car and started the engine.

'Nothing terrible, sweetheart. Went for her usual morning swim and cut her foot on a broken bottle.'

With a judder, he changed up a gear.

'There was a lot of noise over in the cove late last night. Some of those surfers having a party. Litter left everywhere.'

'Is she all right?'

'Doctor put in a few stitches. She has to keep off it for a day or so. She's such a busy soul, too.'

'I'll help her, Grandpa.'

Tom patted her hand.

'I know you will, my love.'

'And Ryan and Cameron can help with the kiln and your pots.'

Anna gripped the edge of her seat as, with a squeal of tyres, the car swerved around a roundabout and on to the Helston road.

'The boys aren't here. Didn't your grandmother tell you?'

'Why not?' Anna said bleakly. 'The twins are always here.'

Tom laughed.

'Well, my love, don't forget, they've just had their eighteenth birthday. Not much fun for them holidaying with their grandparents, is it?'

'There's me here,' Anna said.

'You! You're only a little girl.'

'I'm fourteen, Grandpa.'

She saw the deep lines on Tom's tanned face crinkle.

'I was forgetting. You're almost grown-up.'

'I am grown-up, Grandpa. Everything's quite different since you were young.'

Swinging the car down the hill, past Porthleven, Tom sighed.

'You don't need to tell me that, my love.'

Anna watched the familiar glimpses of sea appear as they travelled, but the excitement they usually brought was gone.

'So where are the boys then?'

'France, with some of their friends. They're touring. Cameron passed his driving test and has a car now.'

'What about Ryan?'

'He's failed the test twice. You can imagine what effect that's had, especially with Cameron passing first time. Ryan doesn't take kindly to being beaten at anything by his brother, as you well know.'

Anna could now see patches of pink heather just breaking into bloom as they crossed Goonhilly Down. A slight mist was drifting in from the sea, covering the windscreen with dampness.

Here, on her own, without the boys! This holiday was going to be dreadful. But Anna had no idea just how terrible it would be . . .

Sally Delabole was still woozy from the painkillers she'd been given. Seeing her, hair untidy and greying, her face pale and lined with weariness, Anna suddenly realised that her grandmother was getting old. She'd never given it a thought before. Sally and Tom had been, to her, unchanging, always there, working on their paintings and pottery, swimming in the sea, laughing with her and the boys.

They were her security. But now . . .

A shiver crept down her back. One day they wouldn't be there.

'Darling!'

Sally opened her arms and Anna was held close, feeling her grandmother's lips kiss the top of her head. Her tense body relaxed.

'Well, darling. We've got you all to ourselves to spoil, until the boys arrive, of course.'

Anna lifted her head, eyes wide and shining.

'So they are coming then?'

'Of course, they are, darling, just for a couple of weeks. They're having a month in France first.'

Anna's shoulders slumped as her grandmother's cheek brushed hers.

'How about us giving them an extra eighteenth birthday party while they're here?'

'On the beach? In the dark? With candles?' Anna burst out.

'Brilliant, darling!'

'When will they arrive?'

Anna counted the days. Four weeks was a long time to spend on her own. There were other young people in the village, but she hardly knew them. Ryan and Cameron had always been there. She didn't need anyone else.

The weather wasn't good either. Damp mist hung in drifts over the cliffs and shrouded the whole countryside. It wasn't picnic weather, not swimming weather either. But then, without the boys, neither would have been much fun.

Anna spent a lot of time in Tom's studio, helping him with his pots. He showed her how to attach handles to mugs and jugs and how to glaze them. She learned how to engrave different names, fire them in the kiln, even paint some of the little models of cottages and inns he produced.

Anna began to look forward to each day with him. He was so different from her father, taking time to show her exactly how to do things. He answered all the many questions she asked, listening to her, letting her experiment with a few designs of her own, and praising the results. He even put her best ideas into production.

'Look at this, Sally,' he said one day, holding out a perfect model of St Michael's Mount. 'The child has natural artistic talent, and we know where that comes from.'

As the weeks passed, she and Sally made preparations for the twins' party, making quiches, sausage rolls, cheesecakes, and her grandmother's special home-made ice-cream. Anna was disappointed to discover it wasn't just to be the five of them.

'They're bringing some of the friends they've been with in France,' Sally told her. 'That's why we need to make so much food and freeze it.'

It was the end of August when they arrived, a week of clear skies and brilliant sunshine that grew hotter as the days progressed.

'Storms are threatened,' Tom warned, his hands deft as he turned a pot on the wheel.

'Not for the party!' Anna cried, leaning forward to watch the wet clay rise up into shape. 'It can't rain for that.'

17

'Hopefully not, but the air's that heavy, I shouldn't be surprised if there's thunder around.'

Anna and Sally were swimming when the boys arrived. Sally's foot had made a good recovery, but she wore light canvas shoes when she went in the water to protect it. It was so hot that even the rocks were too warm to sit on. Anna enjoyed swimming out to a huge slab of granite and perching there, like a mermaid, before making the long haul back to the safety of the beach again.

Hearing the roar of car engines, she left her grandmother to retrieve their towels, and ran across the lane to the house. A battered Range Rover, two ancient Minis and a small van filled the drive when, out of breath, she reached it, and stopped suddenly.

What seemed like hordes of young people were milling about, unloading rucksacks, surfboards, windsurfers.

The gravel was heaped with stuff, and the noise of voices was daunting. Anna's eyes searched for the twins.

'Wowee! Look what the tide's washed up,' a girl's voice drawled. Heads turned.

Anna heard a ripple of laughter and was instantly conscious of her dripping school-regulation navy bathing costume, conscious, too, that since it was bought at the beginning of the year, her body had changed and she was growing out of it.

18

'Who's the kid, Ryan? You never said you had a sister,' a voice she didn't know called out.

Tall, bronzed and, to Anna's eyes, incredibly handsome, Ryan pushed his way through the group.

'Oh, that,' he said, and his mouth twisted into the smile she knew so well. 'Nothing to do with me. Just Anna.'

Anna's teeth bit into her lower lip as her eyes swam with tears.

'Hi, Anna.'

Cameron's arm was round her shoulders, turning her away.

'How's Gran's foot?'

Swallowing, Anna tried to still her quivering mouth.

'Better. We've been swimming. She's down on the beach.'

'Let's go and find her then.'

'Trust Cameron to help a damsel in distress,' Anna heard Ryan say as they walked away, and knew he was still smiling.

*   *   *

After all the preparations, Anna hated the party. It hadn't occurred to her that the group of friends touring France would include girls. Stupid of me, she realised, but here she'd always had the twins to herself.

It was a really hot evening, the air heavy and

difficult to breathe. Everyone went swimming, except Anna. She refused. Even Cameron couldn't persuade her. Two barbecues had been carried across to the beach. Anna could hear their sizzle. The smell of mackerel and sausages mingled, lingering in the sultry air.

She'd watched the sun sink into the sea, its colour sullen. Now the cove was lit with candles, scattered on the rocks. Their flames hardly wavered in the still air. Faces came and went, disappearing into shadow. Anna didn't know any of them—didn't want to.

Tom was controlling one barbecue, turning fish as easily as he turned his pots. The glow from it reflected on his white hair, turning it into a halo. He glanced across and winked at her.

'Come and eat,' Cameron said, sitting on a rock beside her. 'You haven't had anything to eat all evening.'

Anna shook her head. She didn't want to be here. All the excitement of the twins' return was spoiled.

She slid off the rock, moving away into the darkness. Her bare feet sank into the sand. Far out to sea a jag of lightning flickered, and she waited for the thunder.

The far side of the cove was full of shadows. Anna wandered across, leaving the noise of the party behind. She could hear the faint drag of shingle as each wave receded. With her toes lost in wet sand, she stood still, listening, her body tense.

Every so often the sky blazed and the thunder grew louder, making her tremble. Something moved and she spun round, catching her foot on a rock, falling forward. Her hands reached out.

'What the . . .'

Ryan's voice startled her as she touched warm skin. Another voice giggled. In the flare of more lightning, Anna saw Ryan's smile, and the girl entwined with him.

Scrambling to her feet, she turned and ran. Sand flew up, scattering round her. Dry seaweed prickled under her toes. Shells scraped her heels. Across the beach, over the lane, through the garden she ran. A drop of rain splashed her forehead, then another. The storm had broken. Thunder and lightning crashed and crackled around her.

Ahead, Anna could see the shed. Terrified, her wet fingers dragged open the door. Inside, she hunched on a pile of cushions, hearing the patter of rain on the roof. Seeing, every now and then, the windows illuminated.

The party would be over now, with everyone running for shelter . . . and Ryan . . . and that girl.

Thunder crashed right overhead. Anna shut her eyes tight, wrapping her arms round her body. The whole garden was lost in a wall of rain. The cushions were still warm from the sun, soothing her as she buried herself in them. When the storm died away, she slept.

It was the noise that woke her. The door of the shed, it was, banging, blowing to and fro. Anna opened her eyes, and closed them again quickly.

The lightning was back, filling the whole shed. Terror pulsed through her, tensing every muscle.

That noise! That smell!

She lifted her head from the cushions, her eyes suddenly wide. A wall of flame surrounded her, weaving through the dry boards of the shed, twisting towards her. She could feel their heat on her face—just like that time long ago on the beach, when Ryan had forced her face down.

Anna's mouth opened to scream, but no sound came.

CHAPTER THREE

The heat was searing her skin, and smoke was choking her. Anna could see the open doorway, its frame aglow, but no way could she force her limbs to reach it. Then a figure was silhouetted there, head bent, hands stretching out to her.

'Anna!'

'Grandpa! Help me!' she shrieked in terror.

In a swift movement, a wet jacket encircled her face and hair. She felt herself lifted and hurtled forward. With a thud, her body hit the ground, knocking the remaining breath out of her as she rolled sideways into the long, damp grass . . .

Her face was stiff and her skin stung when she next was aware of trying to open her eyes.

Blearily she peered out through a haze of gauze. A beaker brushed her dry lips and a trickle of coolness slipped down her aching throat. She wanted to ask a question, but the words wouldn't form, and she drifted back into darkness.

Sally was there when she woke again. Anna could recognise the shape of her, leaning back in a chair. As Anna moved she bent forward.

'Oh, my poor, little darling.'

Anna opened her mouth and this time the

words whispered out. 'Where's Grandpa?'

Sally's face seemed to crumple and disintegrate, slow tears creeping down, losing themselves in the deep lines furrowing her cheeks. Anna tried to sit up, but the effort was too much and she fell back against the pillows, lost once more in a swirling mist.

Ryan was looking down at her when she finally opened her eyes again. The bones in his face stood out, white, through his tan.

'Our grandfather's dead, Anna. You killed him.'

The fury in his voice bit into her, throbbing through her brain as she struggled to understand.

'Ryan!'

It was Cameron's voice now, angry!

'Stop it! How can you say such a thing!'

'Because it's true! He died saving that stupid, little creature.'

Ryan's face came close to hers.

'Why did you have to break into our lives all those years ago and ruin everything? Why couldn't it be you who's dead?'

'That's enough, Ryan!'

She saw Cameron's nails dig into his brother's shoulder, dragging him away from her. Tears welled behind her eyes and rolled down her cheeks, leaving a trail of pain.

Tom Delabole was dead! That kind, lovely man she called Grandpa. Her mind went back over the last few weeks, the long days they'd spent together in his studio, his patience as he taught her his craft. And now . . .

The ache in her throat couldn't cope with more pain, as sobs shook through her. Cameron's long fingers lightly brushed across her bandaged hand.

'It wasn't your fault, Anna,' he whispered. 'Ryan's upset. We all are. Go to sleep. Get better. We want you home again.'

After that, the questions came. The policewoman spoke to her quietly, but there was no escaping them.

'What were you doing there, Anna? Why did you go to the shed? Did you take candles?'

Anna closed her eyes, and her mind, not wanting to remember. She could still see the glare of the flames, hear the roar as they raced over the dry wood of the shed.

'Anna!'

She didn't want to answer the questions, didn't want to think about what had happened. The picture of Tom, silhouetted in the doorway, was there constantly, no matter how hard she tried to shut it out. And Ryan's bitter words—'Our grandfather's dead, Anna. You killed him.'

'I didn't mean to. I didn't mean to.'

'We know you didn't mean to, Anna,' the woman said. 'But we have to try to find out exactly what happened. Now, tell me. Why were you in the shed? Why weren't you on the beach with the others?'

Anna turned her head away.

'There were candles on the beach, weren't there, Anna? For the party. Did you take some back to the shed? Was there someone else with you? A boy? One of the boys at the party?'

Anna's body stiffened. How could she ask such questions? How could she imply that . . .

'Look, Anna, no-one's going to be angry with you. You're a pretty girl. I'm sure you've plenty of boyfriends. And there was wine, wasn't there? You'd all been drinking. It was a party. Lots of boys and girls together. But you wanted to find somewhere quiet, didn't you?'

The policewoman paused and Anna waited tensely for her to continue.

'The shed was a quiet place. So who was with you, Anna?'

'No-one was with me,' Anna protested. 'I just wanted to be on my own. It was starting to rain, so I went in there. I was scared of the storm, and I just went to sleep.'

'But you had a candle?'

'No!' Anna raged.

'So how did the fire start?'

Anna closed her eyes, trying to escape the probe of the policewoman's steely gaze.

'I don't know, but I didn't have a candle.'

'And you say there was no-one else with you? You can tell me, Anna. I know you're only fourteen, but it was a party. These things happen.'

'I was on my own.'

'All right, Anna. Don't upset yourself. Now tell me what happened when you woke up. The shed was alight?'

Anna nodded.

'But you saw your grandfather?'

The policewoman stopped and gave Anna a questioning look. 'Inside or outside?'

'In the doorway,' Anna replied but her voice was muffled.

'Entering or leaving?'

'He was coming in, coming to help me. And he did! He did! And now he's dead!'

A flood of sobbing overwhelmed her and Sally, who was sitting by the bed, leaned forward to comfort her.

'Must you do this to her?' she pleaded.

'I'm sorry, Mrs Delabole, but we have to get all the details. Would you rather someone else was with her? It must be gruelling for you, too.'

Sally shook her head.

'No, no. She's my granddaughter. I want to be here with her. Are you all right, darling?'

Gulping, Anna nodded.

'Then what happened, Anna?'

'He wrapped something round me. His jacket, I think. It was wet. I couldn't see. And he picked me up and threw me.'

'Threw you?'

'Out through the door. It was burning around the doorway. There were flames everywhere. And then . . .'

Tears choked her voice.

'I don't know what happened then,' she sobbed.

'She's had enough. Please stop now.'

The policewoman closed her notebook.

'I'll talk to her again tomorrow.'

'Do you have to?" Sally asked.

'I'm afraid so. We have to know whether your husband was with her before or after the fire stared, Mrs Delabole.'

'You're not suggesting . . .'

'I'm not suggesting anything, but until I have all the facts, Mrs Delabole, I have to check every possibility.'

Anna thought, years later, that maybe it was a good thing her grandmother had to look after her once she came out of hospital. It gave her something to do, took her mind off her grief. Together they grieved. Maybe that, too, helped them.

Nothing will ever be the same again, Anna realised, as she again sat on the rocks where the boys once fished. This summer is the end of everything. The twins won't come here to stay, now their grandfather is dead. There's no reason to any more. They're eighteen, grown up, leading their own lives. Now there's only Gran and me.

*　　*　　*

28

She didn't return to school that September. It was best for her to recover by the sea, her parents decided. After all, neither of them was free to look after her, whereas her grandmother had time on her hands now.

Anna had never liked September. To her it always signified the end of summer, the time when she and the boys parted and went home for another year. But this year she hated it.

The leaves on the trees were just turning to gold when the gales came, ripping them from the branches. Rain swept in across the cove, to stream down the windows of the house, like tears, Anne thought. It was as though the elements were mourning, too.

With wind roaring down the chimney, making every door in the house rattle, Anna went through into Tom Delabole's studio, built on to the side of the house. It was the first time she'd been there since his death. Everything was just as he'd left it that day.

Together, they'd been painting the little models of St Michael's Mount, the ones Anna had designed, finishing off a batch, before the twins and their friends arrived.

A smell of damp and clay and paint still hung faintly in the chill of the room. Slowly, her gaze travelled round, seeing the row of named mugs waiting on a shelf, ready to be bubble-wrapped and taken to one of the craft shops.

She saw the tall, elegant vases with their sweeping strokes of blue that were Tom's speciality, and the little models of local cottages and inns that he took such care over.

Anna settled herself on Tom's stool and picked up a brush, her tears mingling with the paint as she worked. Later, when Sally found her, Anna was carefully tucking wrapped mugs into a box.

'So this is where you are, darling.'

'I found Grandpa's order book and checked out what's wanted. Tomorrow we can drive over to St Ives and deliver everything. Then, will you help me with the kiln? I think, if I try, I can do some of those vases on the wheel.'

'Anna, darling!'

Anna's chin quivered as she looked up at her grandmother.

'We can't just let all his lovely ideas go to waste, can we? Grandpa would never have wanted that. He spent so much time showing me what to do. And after what happened . . .'

Her voice cracked, and she swallowed before continuing.

'It's up to me now, Gran. I'm going to be a potter, like he was. Will you let me stay here for always?'

Anna's parents were only too pleased when Sally suggested their daughter came to live with her permanently.

'Teenagers are such a responsibility,' her

father said. 'You've so much more time than us, Mother. It'll be company for you, too, now that Tom's gone.'

They'd been to visit her once in hospital, just for an hour.

'So horrific,' they said. 'It upsets us too much to look at her.'

'The burns will heal,' Sally told them abruptly. 'She's young, but she needs your reassurance.'

Cameron had visited her every day, until it was time to return home. He and Ryan were to spend their gap year before university clearing jungle and building huts somewhere in South America. But Ryan never came to see her in hospital.

Anna settled into her new school, knowing it was only for a couple of years. Everyone there knew about the fire and accepted her scarring. Anna was the only one it still troubled.

Her talent for art was encouraged. It was a community where crafts formed the way of life for many of those living there. Cameron wrote occasionally to Sally. After their year abroad, the twins went to university. His letters kept them up to date for a while at least. Still they heard nothing from Ryan.

Anna spent a lot of time in Tom's studio. Everything there reminded her of him. She felt she should have been the one to die, while he worked on, creating beautiful things. No matter how hard she tried, she couldn't produce the lovely vases that were his trademark. Maybe it was right that she shouldn't. After all, they represented Tom, no-one else.

Her little models did well though. At weekends, she and Sally drove to different places, seeking out unusual buildings and well-known landmarks which she photographed or sketched. Her grandmother would sit on a harbour wall or seat somewhere, painting the water colours that sold so rapidly.

'What we need, Gran, is our own shop,' Anna said, pushing back the heavy sweep of dark hair that hid one cheek.

She was almost twenty now and coming to the end of an art course at one of the local colleges.

'It's silly to let someone else take half our profit. Do you think we could get planning permission to convert one of the rooms?'

'I'm too old for that sort of venture, darling.'

'Of course you're not, Gran. Nobody's old nowadays. All you'd have to do is carry on painting.'

Anna's smile widened.

'In fact, you could be the demonstration model. You know how, whenever you're out painting, people always hover round, trying to watch. Well, if you sat in the window, working, that would draw them in. What d'you think?'

'Oh, Anna!'

'It's a great idea, Gran! Please say yes. I'll have to find a job when I finish the course and this would solve everything.'

Sally pursed her lips.

'Well,' she said slowly, 'I suppose we could convert the studio. Then use you for demonstration purposes as well!'

'Let's find out then.'

Anna decided that while she was on a visit to Truro, taking photographs of the cathedral for one of her new models, she'd find out what had to be done about converting the studio. In the distance, on her way there, a helicopter wove its way along the coastline as she drove off the Lizard Peninsula and followed the road, past Helston. Soon this road would be crowded with tourists heading for the beaches, but now it shouldn't be too difficult to find somewhere to park in Truro.

Less than an hour later, she was trying to work out how she could angle her camera. The cathedral fitted so tightly into the narrow streets, that it was impossible to stand far enough back to get it all in. Eventually, Anna found she could take a good view of its three spires by standing on the top floor of the carpark where she'd left the car.

With such beautiful sunshine, it was too nice a day to spend inside a stuffy restaurant, so she then bought some sandwiches and sat on a seat in the nearby shopping precinct to eat them.

She was just about to drop the plastic wrapping in a bin when her hand stilled. Her gaze fixed on the man walking towards her. He was tall, leanly built, dark hair tousled.

Anna's breath caught in her throat and her heart began to pound. It was six years since she'd seen the twins. Was this Ryan or Cameron heading towards her?

CHAPTER FOUR

Anna didn't know what to do. For the past few years they'd heard nothing from either of the twins. Even Cameron's letters had died away.

None of us had anything in common, Anna thought. Without Tom there was nothing to hold us together.

The man had almost reached her now. Any moment he'd pass. Quickly she smoothed her hair over one cheek, and stepped out in front of him. Avoiding a collision, he stopped, and she saw him frown.

'Anna?'

His blue eyes. were puzzled. Even then she wasn't sure which twin it was.

'Anna, it is you! You've grown-up. I hardly recognised you.'

His arms closed round her in a hug. She buried her face in the shoulder of his navy sweatshirt. This could only be Cameron.

'It is six years,' she said, lifting her head to look at him.

He sighed.

'Is it really that long? Are you still living round here? I thought, by now, you'd be working away somewhere. And your grandmother? Is she . . .'

'Still alive?' Anna said, drily. 'Yes.'

He looked down at the empty wrapper in

her hand.

'Have you eaten? How about a coffee? We've such a lot to catch up on.'

'How's . . .'

'Ryan? Oh, he's fine. Getting married, to a lovely girl, Laura. Shall we try this place? The coffee smells good.'

So it was Cameron! Anna released her breath slowly. It had to be. Ryan would never have greeted her like that.

After they'd carried their coffee to a table, Anna studied him carefully, seeing that anxious, rather serious expression she remembered so well. There were faint lines etching away from his eyes now. His face was slightly more thin, but his eyes were just as blue and his hair as dark as ever.

'Sugar?'

He took a coloured packet from the bowl on the table and offered it to her. Anna shook her head.

'I don't. Have you forgotten?'

'It's been a long time,' he said.

'You stopped writing your letters to us.'

'No-one ever wrote back to me.'

'Gran did, didn't she?'

Anna sounded surprised.

'No, and you certainly didn't.'

'I thought . . .'

She paused and looked at him over the rim of her cup.

'I thought you hated me as much as Ryan,

after what happened.'

'And I thought you wanted to forget all about us. Too many memories.'

'Most of them were nice ones, Cameron. It was only that summer. Everything changed then.'

He reached across the table and put his hand over hers.

'I'm sorry.'

'So what are you doing now?' she asked quickly, drawing her hand away.

'Oh, this and that.'

'Cameron!'

He smiled. So different from Ryan's smile, Anna thought. It changed his face completely, and she could see the boy he used to be.

'Well, I eventually qualified as an architect. Probably some of Grandpa's love of detail in my genes. To start with, it was designing horrid little boxes for housing estates. I hated that.'

'So?' she prompted, as he drained his cup.

'I set up on my own, restoring old properties. Conservation, I suppose you'd call it.'

'Sounds good.'

'It all takes time. I shall never be a millionaire. More coffee? There's some left in the pot.'

'And Ryan?' she said, not looking at him as she poured. 'What's he doing? Apart from getting married, that is.'

'Oh, you know Ryan. Has to be at the top.

He works for one of the big estate agencies as a surveyor. Making a fortune, he is.'

'And the girl he's marrying?'

Cameron gave a rueful laugh.

'Laura doesn't do a lot. Officially she's personal assistant to her father, a very wealthy man. Sort of lord of the manor. Has a big estate in North Devon, near Bideford. Stately home, open to the public twice a week. Laura deals with all that.'

'You don't sound too impressed.'

'Don't I? Sorry. It's just that they're a bit over-the-top for me, and Ryan's becoming like them.'

Time to change the subject, Anna decided.

'So what are you doing in Truro?

Leaning back in his chair, Cameron relaxed slightly.

'There's a property being auctioned over near Helston. It's an old farmhouse. Rumour has it the intention is to pull it down and put a caravan site there. Thought I'd have a look at it.'

'A caravan site? That's lowering your standards a bit, isn't it?'

Cameron leaned forward again.

'That wouldn't be my idea at all. From the photos, it was once a lovely, old house. Seems a pity if it were destroyed.'

Anna finished her coffee and picked up her bag.

'Helston's on my way home. Can I come and

look at it with you?'

He raised one eyebrow.

'Sure?'

'Positive,' she said. 'Do you know anything about planning permission for conversions, by the way?'

Guiding her towards the door, Cameron laughed.

'One of my specialities. Where have you parked your car?'

It was good to be back in his company again . . .

It was almost as though we've never been apart, Anna thought, standing at the end of a muddy lane, watching Cameron's face as he studied the dilapidated building. Several of the sash windows were shattered, either by weather or vandals. Once their frames had been white, now only flakes of paint were left. Slates hung loose in places on the roof and the guttering drooped.

'Do you want to see inside?' he asked.

Is it worth it, Anne wondered, but nodded.

Cameron had to put his shoulder to the door, easing it forward when it stuck. A smell of dankness and dirt met them as they stepped into the panelled hallway. Anna was surprised to see a wide, wooden staircase leading upwards from what she guessed to be a black and white tiled floor, under all the grime and mud.

'Careful, it's a bit dark,' Cameron warned,

as he began to climb.

The whole house was far bigger than she expected. Upstairs, the high ceilings of the rooms were trailed with cobwebs. Anna let out a shriek as one, long and black, drifted across her face before draping itself over Cameron's hair.

She watched as he paced the rooms, measuring and tapping walls, stamping on floorboards, jotting down details in a notebook.

'This bathroom's archaic! Blue willow-patterned toilet and wash-basin,' Anna said, wiping a finger across the dusty edge. 'Very grand. And look at that huge bath, with feet!'

Back downstairs, Cameron examined the fireplace in the main room, prising a wooden panel slightly away with a penknife. His breath whistled out.

'If only I could move this a bit more. I'm sure it's covering up something far larger. And that ceiling! It looks to me as though it's been put in to block off one higher up.'

'But why?' Anna asked, frowning.

'Whoever bought this place, years ago, needed it smaller and warmer. Think of all the heat wasted by rising up to fill ceiling space. And who'd want a huge fireplace? It would need piles of logs or coal. No, I think there's far more to this house than meets the eye.'

'But someone must have noticed.'

Cameron brushed dust and cobwebs from

the front of his sweatshirt.

'I'm sure someone has. If I'm right, then all the hidden fittings are worth a lot. So, if the house is pulled down, out they'll come and be sold on. That bathroom suite alone would fetch hundreds.'

He wrinkled his nose and sneezed.

'It may have been a farmhouse for donkey's years, but I'm positive there's more history to it than that. I'd need to go over it more thoroughly, but from what I've seen so far, I wouldn't be surprised if the original building isn't sixteenth century.'

'But no-one would pull it down if it was, surely?'

'Selling off the land would raise a lot more money than it would take to restore this place, Anna.'

'So what are you going to do about it?'

Cameron smoothed a finger down the side of her cheek.

'Bid for it! The auction's tomorrow.'

As his hand touched her skin, Anna pulled away, shaking her hair forward in a swift movement. He frowned.

'What's wrong?'

She turned her head away, but he caught her shoulders, swinging her round to face him again, and stared down at her in the gloom of the hallway.

'Is it that scar that worries you? From the fire?'

With gentle hands he lifted the curtain of hair and lightly kissed her cheek.

'It's so ugly,' she said hurriedly, embarrassed by his scrutiny.

'You will never be ugly, Anna. I'm quite sure no-one notices it, except you.'

'But they do,' she insisted. 'Their eyes immediately fix on it. It happens all the time.'

'Nonsense, Anna. You're being far too sensitive. It's the person people see, not what they look like.'

'Few bother to take a second look.'

'Oh, Anna!' he said, putting his arm round her shoulders and hugging her. 'Maybe you don't give them the chance. Come on, let's go. We've seen enough here. And I must get back to Truro.'

'Must you?'

Cameron hesitated.

'I'm booked into a hotel overnight.'

'Phone and say you've changed your plans. Gran will be upset if you don't stay with us.'

'But my case is there. Pyjamas . . . razor.'

Anna laughed.

'You can collect them tomorrow, after the auction. And you must have a razor, your grandfather's is still in a drawer. If you remember, Gran never throws anything away.'

*   *   *

It's almost like it used to be, Anna thought,

watching Sally fussing round Cameron, pouring tea, while a casserole simmered on the Aga. Almost, but not quite. There was no Tom, and no Ryan.

'So Ryan's getting married,' Sally said, as if reading Anna's mind. 'It seems no time ago I was having to chase him round the tea table when he refused to wash his hands after delving in rock pools.'

Cameron laughed.

'I dare say Laura will be doing that in future. She's a bit fastidious.'

Sally sorted out knives and forks, and laid them on the table.

'Lives out near Bideford, did you say? Not all that far from here, is it? When's the wedding going to be?'

Cameron put his arm round her waist and hugged her.

'I'm sorry, Gran, but I can't see you getting an invitation now. They were sent out weeks ago.'

Sally's chin thrust forward.

'And we don't expect one, do we, Anna?'

'There's nothing to stop Ryan inviting you, Gran, but somehow I don't think I'd be on the list.'

'Like a little sister, you were, my darling.'

Anna's mouth curved into a rueful smile.

'I don't think Ryan ever liked me much.'

'Only because you put his nose out of joint,' Cameron said quietly. 'He was Grandpa's

43

favourite until you came along.'

'And did I put your nose out of joint, too?' she asked, twisting the edge of a serviette round her finger.

'No, Anna. I fell under your spell instantly.'

'Well, who wouldn't?' Sally said, glancing thoughtfully from one to the other. 'She was a little poppet, wasn't she? Now, mind these plates. They've just come out of the oven.'

Next morning, Sally decided to join Anna and Cameron at the auction.

'Couldn't stay away, could I, after all I've heard about the place? The pair of you never stopped chattering on for half the night.'

She peered out through the side window of the car.

'That's not the house, is it? That tumbledown heap?'

Several vans and cars were already scattered around the muddy yard. With Cameron leading the way, Anna and her grandmother stepped carefully towards the open farmhouse door. A very mixed group was crowded into the main room downstairs. Some were dark-suited, looking out of place among the rest wearing well-worn anoraks or wax jackets and heavily-muddied green wellingtons.

'Quite sure you want to join this?' Cameron asked, as they were pushed against the wall by others cramming in.

'Couldn't escape now, even if we wanted to,' Sally said with a chuckle.

By standing on her toes, Anna could see that an old bench had been placed at the far end of the room, in front of the fireplace. A heavily-built, florid-faced man was being helped, with some difficulty because of his size, to stand on it.

'That's the auctioneer,' Cameron breathed into her ear.

'I had realised,' Anna protested.

'What's happening, darling?' her grandmother asked. 'I can't see a thing for that man's hat in front. Can you give him a prod and ask him to take it off?'

Anna frowned at her.

'Of course not, Gran.'

'From the state of it, it's probably never left his head since the day he bought it, at a jumble sale, no doubt,' Sally retorted.

'Ssh, Gran! The auctioneer's about to start.'

Anna had never been to an auction before.

'Right then, ladies and gentlemen,' the auctioneer said. 'Let's make a start, shall we? We have on offer today one lot only, Trevellion Farm, to be sold with its entire contents and surrounding land. I dare say you've all read the details and been round the property. Now, who'd like to start the bidding?'

Anna couldn't believe the speed at which the price rose and then began to slow when it reached one hundred thousand ponds. So far, Cameron hadn't made a bid.

'I thought you wanted it,' she hissed in his ear.

'Be patient. I don't want to push the price up by showing I'm keen.'

'Come along, ladies and gentlemen. One hundred thousand pounds. A ridiculous price for such a property. Do I hear one hundred and one? You, sir?'

The auctioneer nodded in Cameron's direction. Anna was surprised. She hadn't seen him move.

'Two . . . three . . . four . . . five. That's more like it, ladies and gentlemen.'

'Who's bidding against Cameron?' Sally whispered.

'Can't see, Gran. Someone near the door, I think.'

'One ten.'

The bidding was rising rapidly again now. Anna glanced anxiously up at Cameron. His whole face was taut. Can he afford to keep going higher, she wondered. Everyone else had dropped out. It was just between Cameron and the person by the door. Anna stood on tiptoe and strained to see who it was. That wretched man's hat's in the way, she fumed, trying to see round him.

Surely it's not that auburn-haired girl? From the way she's dressed, I'm amazed she put her nose inside the door of this cobwebby place.

'One ninety.'

The auctioneer waited, gavel raised, as his

gaze veered across the room to Cameron. Anna's teeth dug into her lip.

'Thank you, sir. Two hundred thousand.'

Cameron let out a long, slow breath.

'And that's it as far as I'm concerned. I can't go any higher,' he murmured in Anna's ear.

She caught hold of his arm and squeezed it. Surely no-one would bid higher. It was a stupid price in any case for such a ruin. The man in the hat was pushing his way out of the crowd, towards the door. Anna saw the auburn-haired girl step aside to let him go through. Her heartbeat quickened.

She knew, now, who was bidding against Cameron. It wasn't the girl, but the tall, handsome, dark-haired man standing next to her. The auctioneer directed his gaze towards him.

'Two hundred and twenty-five thousand pounds. Thank you, sir. Any advance on two hundred and twenty-five thousand pounds?'

From the doorway on the other side of the room, the bidder looked across at Cameron, and smiled mockingly.

It was a smile Anna had never forgotten.

CHAPTER FIVE

Ryan! Of all the people bidding against Cameron, it had to be Ryan. What on earth is he doing here, Anna wondered. And then she remembered Cameron had told her that Ryan was a surveyor and worked for a large estate agency.

He'd also told her of the intention to pull down the farmhouse and use the land for a caravan park. Was that Ryan's idea?

The whole room was silent now. It was as though everyone had stopped breathing. Necks turned slowly towards Cameron, waiting. Anna watched his shoulders slump as he shook his head.

'No bid, sir? Right then. Two hundred and twenty-five thousand pounds I'm bid. Going . . . going . . .'

There was a flurry of movement next to Anna and her grandmother's hand shot up in the air, waving frantically.

'Two hundred and fifty thousand!' she shouted at the top of her voice. 'That should stop him!'

'Gran!' Anna cried. 'You don't know what you're doing!'

'Oh, yes, I do,' Sally replied calmly.

'You haven't got that much money, Gran.'

'Don't worry, darling. Cameron was

prepared to go to two hundred thousand. I shall just put up the remaining fifty.'

'But where from, Gran?'

'Darling, I said don't worry.'

A great wave of clapping filled the room. The auctioneer repeated Sally's bid, looked in the direction of Ryan and then Cameron, and finally banged down his gavel, there being no other bids forthcoming.

'Sold to Mrs Delabole.'

'How does he know your name, Gran?' Anna asked.

Sally shrugged.

'Matthew Trevose? Oh, we've met.'

She took hold of Anna's arm.

'Come on. Let's go and have a drink somewhere. All this dust and excitement has left me dry.'

'I don't know what to say, Gran.'

Cameron looked dazed as Sally seized his arm, too.

'After all you said about the place! A tumbledown heap, wasn't that it? What's made you decide . . .'

'I like your ideas. You're right, there's more to this house than being demolished and a field of caravans put in its place. We Cornish need to hang on to our heritage.'

'All together again, eh? Just like old times.'

Ryan's voice held a hint of sarcasm as he sauntered over to them. 'Let me introduce Laura, my future bride.'

Anna's body stiffened as Ryan's fingers dug into her elbow.

'I've told her a lot about you.'

'All good, I hope,' Sally observed drily.

Ryan's gaze was on Anna as he smiled and a tremor went through her.

'With exceptions,' he replied, 'with exceptions. Now, let me take you all for a drink to celebrate your purchase, Gran. What a dark horse you are. I had no idea you were interested in the property market. What do you intend to do with the place, now you own it?'

'I need to settle things with Matthew Trevose first. Cameron, will you come with me?'

Sally turned to Anna.

'Go along with Ryan and Laura, darling. We'll meet you all in The Smugglers. Ask if it's not too late for lunch, will you?'

'Well, Anna,' Ryan murmured against her ear, as he guided her into the back seat of his car. 'We meet again. I see you still bear the scars to remind you of my grandfather's death.'

Tugging the seat-belt round her, Anna shook a veil of hair round her face, and her chin jutted.

'It was never discovered exactly how the blaze started, Ryan. Maybe it was someone who liked starting little fires.'

'Don't start on all that again, Ryan, sweetheart. Besides, it's ancient history now,'

Laura said, slamming the car door with some force. 'And I'm sure you don't want to be reminded of it, do you, Anna? It must have been a terrible ordeal for you, being burned like that.'

Aware of Laura's perfect creamy skin, Anna tugged a strand of hair more closely across her cheek. Cameron was so wrong, she thought. It is the first thing people notice.

Reflected in the driving mirror, she saw Ryan's face, and his smile.

What am I doing here, she asked herself. Why didn't I insist on staying with Cameron and Gran?

Through the window she saw high, grassy banks rise on either side of the car, topped by stone walls almost hidden by tufts of pink thrift. A few remaining bluebells, mingled with red campion and the occasional tall foxglove, swayed in the breeze from the sea. Everywhere was so beautiful at this time of year. What a pity it had to be spoiled by being in Ryan's company, Anna thought.

From The Smugglers there was a clear view straight across fields to the sea, stretching way out into the hazy distance.

'Let's sit outside until the others come,' Laura suggested, dumping her bag on a wooden bench and taking out a packet of cigarettes. 'It's glorious with all these roses. You go in and order, Ryan. What'll it be, Anna?'

'Oh, cider. I think they brew their own. It's very good anyway.'

'Then I'll have the same. You'd better use a tray, sweetheart.'

Anna saw his lips tighten slightly, and remembered that Ryan never liked being told what to do.

'So what do you do, Anna?' Laura asked.

'Gran and I are about to open a craft shop. She paints and I make a few pots. We're hoping to convert Tom's old studio.'

'Tom?'

'Ryan's grandfather.'

'The one who died, you mean?'

Anna nodded.

'Do tell me what happened. I've only ever heard Ryan's version, and, of course, he's terribly biased. Blames you for everything.'

'I don't really know what did happen,' Anna said. 'I was asleep in the shed and . . .'

She shuddered at the memory.

'And when I woke up, it was on fire.'

'How frightful for you,' Laura drawled. 'You must have been absolutely frantic. You were only twelve, weren't you?'

'Fourteen.'

'I gather there'd been a beach party. Someone's birthday or something, wasn't it? Ryan said you were drunk and had taken candles into the shed with you. That's what started the fire.'

Anna looked at her in horror.

'I wasn't drunk! I didn't have anything to eat or drink at the party. And I certainly didn't take any candles. Didn't Ryan tell you there was a thunderstorm? It could have been lightning striking the shed. No-one really knows.'

'Except you, Anna.'

Ryan was behind them, carefully balancing three glasses in his hands. 'And you're not likely to confess, are you?'

'We shall cease this conversation and talk about something entirely different,' Laura announced, taking one of the glasses. 'Oh, Ryan, it's spilled all down the side. Why didn't you use a tray, like I said?'

'Did you ask about lunch?' Anna asked, hoping to divert a squabble.

'Of course.'

Ryan seated himself close beside her. She tried to edge away but the end of the bench prevented her.

'So what's on offer?' Laura asked.

'Not a lot at this time of day. Mainly salad with a choice of smoked mackerel, salmon, ham or cheese or the usual jacket potatoes filled with whatever they've got. Oh, and there's an omelette. All the specials are off. What else can you expect from a back-of-beyond shack like this?'

'Gran likes it, Ryan. She used to come here a lot with Tom.'

Ryan swallowed half his drink.

'So it's going to be a trip down memory lane, is it? Marvellous!'

A teenage girl in T-shirt and jeans came out to the table, and hovered, notepad in hand.

'Would you like to order, sir? Only it's getting a bit late and we don't do lunches after two o'clock.'

'No, we wouldn't! For goodness' sake!' Ryan said, glowering at her. 'With the choice you've got on the menu, it's not going to take long to slap it on the plates, is it? And there are still two more people to come.'

Frowning, the girl chewed her lip and rubbed one sandalled foot against the other. Anna stood up.

'It's all right, I can see the others driving in. I'll go and hurry them along.' Anything, she decided, to escape Ryan's bad manners.

Anna grasped her grandmother's elbow and helped her out of the car.

'Thank goodness you've arrived. We need to order quickly.'

Sally gave her a kiss.

'Sorry, darling. It all took longer than we expected, didn't it, Cameron? Now, tell me what's on the menu as we walk. The crab's usually very good. Locally caught.'

It was a meal Anna preferred to forget. The atmosphere was electric. Ryan started to question Sally as soon as the meal arrived.

'Should you really be wasting your money, buying that wreck of a place, Gran? What on earth are you going to do with it? It's only fit to be demolished.'

'It's really none of your business, Ryan,' Sally replied sharply and turned towards Anna. 'This crab is absolutely delicious, darling. Caught locally, you know. What's your mackerel like?'

Ryan leaned across the table.

'If my grandfather hadn't married you, everything in his will would have gone to Cameron and me. But instead, you and dear little Anna . . .'

Anna's head jerked up as Ryan went on.

'I'm sure you were both delighted when he died so conveniently.'

The table shook, glasses spilling, as Sally stood up, throwing down her serviette, her eyes narrowing.

'How dare you, Ryan!'

She pulled her jacket more closely round her and, with shaking hands, struggled to do up the buttons.

'Cameron, will you drive us home? Now, please.'

'Oh, Mrs Delabole, please, don't go.'

Laura reached out to touch Sally's arm.

'Ryan, sweetheart, you must apologise. He's just a bit upset, you see. What with the forthcoming wedding and now this auction and losing that property. It's stress, isn't it, darling?'

'Laura!' Ryan spat out the name. 'Shut up!'

55

There was silence in the car as Cameron drove away up the lane. Anna could see her grandmother's back, straight and stiff, in the seat in front of her.

'I'm so sorry, Gran,' Cameron almost whispered.

'It was my own fault, Cameron. I should have realised. Getting you all together like that, it was stupid of me. But I thought, after all this time . . .'

'I'm afraid my brother will never change, Gran. And he did think an awful lot of our grandfather.'

'So did you, Cameron, but you're not bitter, are you?'

'It was an accident, Gran. That I do know, and we all suffered.'

He glanced up into the driving mirror, meeting Anna's gaze.

'And Anna has suffered more than the rest of us.'

'What did Ryan mean about the will, Gran?' Anna asked, once they were home and Cameron had gone.

'Tom left everything to me for the rest of my life, then it all goes to you. He loved you very much, you know.'

'But what about the twins?'

'I have the option of making bequests to them, if I choose. The bulk of his estate will go to you, though. You'll be quite a wealthy young lady.'

'But I thought . . .'

Sally laughed.

'You thought we were as poor as church mice? Not so. Tom was very knowledgeable about art. He picked up a few bargains over the years. It's surprising what can turn up at jumble sales or auctions. That's how I know Matthew Trevose. Tom bought and sold, made investments.'

Anna felt stunned.

'I could have purchased that old farm straight off, but it wouldn't have been fair to Cameron. He's an independent young man. Always has been.'

She patted Anna's cheek.

'No, I'm quite prepared to help him out for the time being, but he's insistent on paying me back as soon as possible. That's why we were a bit late. He wanted to have it all cut and dried legally.'

'Do the twins know just how wealthy their grandfather left you? And what is to happen when you . . .'

Anna couldn't finish what she'd been saying.

'It was no secret. Tom was quite open about everything. He didn't mention it to you, of course. Considered you were still a child.'

'But they did know everything was to be left to you, and then me, after Tom died?' Anna persisted.

Sally nodded.

'They both knew about the amount of

money he made from art sales, too. Often went with him.'

'But why leave it to me, and not them?'

'Oh, Tom was like that, a bit old-fashioned. Considered it character-building for boys to struggle a bit and make their own way in the world, as he himself did.'

'But not me?'

'I said your grandfather had old-fashioned ideals, darling. Thought that all females should be loved and cherished. Hence, the pair of us . . .'

Anna bit her lower lip, her mind churning, trying to push away the thoughts that were forming. The twins both knew that eventually Tom's fortune would come to her. She shut her eyes, not wanting to imagine any more. Her brain spun on.

If I had died in that fire, they would have inherited. Only the fire didn't kill me. Instead it killed their grandfather.

And Gran and I still stood between them and all his money.

CHAPTER SIX

Did that mean one, or maybe both of the twins set fire to the shed, Anna asked herself, to eliminate me?

But that was six years ago now. Why hadn't they tried again? Or did what happened to their grandfather bring them to their senses?

I'm being stupid, Anna thought, letting my imagination run away with me. The fire was an accident. Nothing was ever discovered that could point to arson. It could only have been the lightning that evening.

'It'll be good having Cameron here with us again, won't it?' Sally said, putting the kettle on to boil. 'Like old times.'

'It won't be for long though, Gran. Just while he's getting the restoration of the farmhouse underway.'

Dropping two teabags into the pot, her grandmother smiled.

'I wouldn't be surprised if he's here quite a bit in future. Now that Ryan's about to be married, I dare say Cameron will want to follow suit.'

She lifted the kettle from the stove and began to pour.

'And I can't help noticing the way he looks at you.'

'Don't be silly, Gran! Cameron's known me

for years. I'm like a sister to him and Ryan. You said so yourself.'

Sally put the lid back on the teapot and took a couple of mugs from their hooks.

'Ah, but you're not his sister, are you?'

Anna's trembling fingers slipped under the waterfall of dark hair to touch her cheek.

'There's no way any man would look twice at someone with a face like this.'

'Oh, darling!'

Sally's arms folded round Anna's stiff body.

'You worry too much about that scar. I've told you so many times that people don't notice it any more. You're the only one who is conscious of it now.'

'Laura commented on it, Gran. So did Ryan.'

'Knowing Ryan, I dare say he was just being his usual unpleasant self. How two boys can be so different, I'll never understand. I suppose that's what identical twins are like, completely opposite sides of each other.' She tipped milk into the mugs and added the tea.

'As for Laura, I can't judge yet. Now, drink up and we'll start making plans for converting Tom's studio. Cameron's given us so much information about planning permission and everything.'

*　　*　　*

Anna and her grandmother were returning

across the lane from the cove after a morning swim, when they saw the postman about to walk up their path.

'Just the one, Mrs Delabole. Very expensive-looking envelope. What's the sea like down there today? Bit chilly, isn't it?'

'Yes, it was, Jim, which is why we're in a rush to get back indoors and dry off properly. Thank you. Goodbye,' Sally said, unlocking the door.

'That was a bit rude of you, Gran. He was dying to see who it's from.'

Sally laughed.

'And have the details all round the village in five minutes? I've known Jim since he was knee-high. Always a chatter-box.'

'Well, I'm curious, too, Gran. Go on, open it.'

Wrapping the beach towel round her body like a sarong, Sally brushed sand from her fingers, picked up a knife and slit open the flap.

'Oh, very elaborate,' she said, taking out a large gold-edged card.

Silently, she read it, then handed it to Anna.

'Ryan's and Laura's wedding. We're both invited, darling. Shall we say we're doing something else that day?'

'Lie, you mean, Gran?'

'Why not? You only have to look at the invitation to know the whole affair will be way out of our class. Nobody will notice whether we're there or not. Is that the phone? Be a darling and answer it, will you? I must dry my hair or it'll be like straw.'

Obediently, Anna picked up the receiver.

'Oh, hello, Laura. Yes, it's just arrived.'

She paused, and raised her eyebrows questioningly at her grandmother.

'Can I ring you back? We've just come in from a swim and we're dripping all over the floor. Until she looks in her diary, Gran isn't sure whether we're already doing something that day or not. OK. About ten minutes.'

'Checking up on us, is she, darling?'

'Don't be so horrid, Gran. Laura sounded quite genuine. We must come, she said. Ryan has so few in his family and she has so many that the seating in the church will look unequal.'

'You mean we're only invited to even up the sides of the church a little?'

Anna laughed.

'I don't think Laura meant it quite like that. She really did sound as though she wanted us to be there.'

Sally began to towel her hair vigorously.

'I'll think about it.'

'You've only five minutes left to do so then. Don't forget, I said I'd ring her back.'

They were halfway up the stairs when the phone rang again.

'She's either impatient or desperate,' Sally murmured, as Anna ran back down to answer it.

'Cameron! Yes, we have. Gran's making up her mind. You speak to her then. She might take some notice of you.'

Anna held out the receiver to Sally.

'It's Cameron. Says he wants us there for support. He's best man.'

She sat on the bottom stair, listening to one side of the conversation, until her grandmother ended up saying, 'I doubt we shall even come into contact with you if you're best man. But if it makes you feel there's at least someone on your side, then I suppose we'll have to be there. You do realise it's moral blackmail though, don't you, Cameron?'

'So we are going then, Gran?'

Sally nodded.

'It'll mean posh frocks. Anyway, we can combine that with a trip to Truro and sort out the planning permission at the same time.'

She began to climb the stairs.

'I suppose we shall have to invite the boys' parents to stay with us. Do you mind if I use the shower first? I'll be as quick as I can.'

'Of course not, Gran.'

Anna perched herself on the bathroom stool.

'What are they like, the parents? They never seemed to be around whenever I was here.'

She heard the water begin to flow and her grandmother's reply was muffled.

'I only met them a couple of times. Father was in the army, always in some foreign place or other. She used to go with him. Devoted to each other, Tom said. That's why the twins were at boarding school. Oh, that's better. I feel human again. Now, I'll prepare something to eat while you return the call to Laura—before I change my mind!'

'You'll be staying here for the weekend,' Laura informed Anna, when they spoke. 'There's heaps of room and it'll save you a rush on the day.'

'Well, I'm not . . .'

'Don't argue, Anna. Ryan insists.'

'He won't be staying as well, will he? I mean, the bride and groom shouldn't meet on the day until the wedding ceremony, should they? It's unlucky or something.'

'Oh, Anna, don't be so old-fashioned! With everybody living together, what does it matter any more? No, you'll arrive on the Friday and leave Sunday. I'll drop the wedding list in the post. See you then. Goodbye.'

'So there!' Anna told her grandmother. 'We've had our orders.'

Sally tucked a strand of straying grey hair back into her pony-tail.

'Oh no! That means dressing-up for a whole weekend. I said we shouldn't go.'

Cameron returned a few days later. Anna was in the studio working at the wheel, when she heard car tyres crunch over the gravel outside. The vase she was working on wobbled, leaned sideways and collapsed. Abandoning it, Anna wiped her hands down the sides of her overall and ran to meet him.

When she reached the door, she slowed, remembering what Gran had said about the way Cameron looked at her. But then, she thought, some people's mothers and grandmothers are like that—matchmaking, reading something into nothing, wishful thinking. But, sadly life isn't like that any more. Even so, she was very conscious of Cameron's arms hugging her and the kiss that avoided the cheek she offered, and met her lips instead. Abruptly, she pulled away.

'What's wrong?' he asked, hauling his case from the car boot and catching hold of her elbow.

'Nothing,' she replied, walking stiffly beside him.

'Is everything sorted out with Ryan and Laura now?' he said, steering her through the doorway. 'Can you imagine what it'll be like, staying in a stately home? D'you suppose we have to dress for dinner, with butlers and staff to wait on us?'

Her shoulders relaxed a little as she laughed.

'How do you imagine Ryan fits into that sort of life? He hates to conform.'

'Oh, Ryan will be loving it. He's changed quite a bit since we were all here with the grandparents. Always had an eye for being at the top, though, didn't he? Am I still in the usual room?'

Anna nodded.

'Where else? Same old bunk beds. You know what Gran's like. Hates parting with anything. That room hasn't changed since you and Ryan slept there as children. But then, you know that from when you were here last time.'

'Stay and talk to me, while I unpack.'

'No, I'll go down and put on the kettle. Gran's driven over to St Ives with a couple of water colours for one of the craft shops there. She should be back soon and she'll be dying for a cup of tea.'

'Any chance of a swim? It was baking in the car.'

'If you're quick.'

'Come with me then.'

'Well . . .'

'Please, Anna. Leave the kettle on low. Gran can make her own tea. She won't mind. Let's swim out to your mermaid rock. Do you remember how you used to sit on it when you were little, coming your long hair with your fingers and pretending to swish your tail?'

'And Gran used to be really cross with me, when she had to brush out all the tangles,' Anna said, laughing as she leaned against the door-jamb.

'I'll give you five minutes to get changed, then race you to the beach.'

With a towel draped round his shoulders, Cameron was already downstairs and filling the kettle when Anna joined him in the kitchen. She watched his eyes scan over her.

'That's definitely an improvement on the navy blue school bathing costume you were wearing the day when . . .'

His voice trailed away.

'When your grandfather died. Is that what you were going to say?'

'It's a time best forgotten. I'm sorry for mentioning it, Anna. Come on, let's go. Last one to the beach makes the tea when we get back, and you're not having a head-start just because you're the youngest.'

Anna had almost forgotten that challenge, something the boys always said when they were children, started, she felt quite sure, by Ryan. It was the sort of thing he would say, knowing she'd never catch them up.

Swiftly, she followed, Cameron's long legs striding ahead of her, sand flying up as they reached the cove. In a flurry of spray, they swam side by side, until Cameron surged forward and was hauling himself up on to the rock by the time she arrived. He leaned down, one hand held out to her, and landed with a terrific splash as she jerked him in and had climbed up before he spluttered to the surface again.

'That's cheating,' he said, laughing, and grabbed her foot, dragging her in as well.

67

'Don't forget, Cameron, all's fair in . . .'

Anna stopped abruptly. Cameron's arms closed round her, pulling her against his body, as he trod water.

'All's fair in what, Anna? Love and war?' he said, and the pupils of his eyes were so dark she could only see a rim of blue. 'You and I will never be at war.'

A wave swept in, curling over their heads, dragging them down into its depths. Panic-stricken, Anna clung desperately to Cameron's shoulders. With a kick of his feet, they both rose to the surface, gasping. He lifted her on to the rock and then swung himself up beside her, his arm round her.

'Are you OK?'

Cameron always seems to be asking me that, she thought, even when we were children. Her mind went back to that day on the beach when she was six, with her sandcastle, the fire, and Ryan's fingers pressing into the back of her neck, forcing her over it. Slowly, she turned her face towards Cameron.

His palm cupped her chin, tilting it. She saw his lips part slightly, before his mouth touched hers, and then she was lost in the depth of his kiss. It was how she'd always imagined a kiss should be.

Sun burned into her skin, or was it the warmth of Cameron's body, she wondered. Her fingers smoothed the nape of his neck, and she heard his breathing quicken as his kiss intensified. She wasn't sure if the pounding she could hear was her own heartbeat or his, or both pulsing together. Or was it just the sea, beating against the rock?

They finally pulled away from each other, breathless.

'Gran'll be back,' Anna whispered, her mouth still hovering close to his.

He kissed her again gently, then tugged her to her feet, their bodies leaning together, reluctant to part.

'Don't forget, last one to the beach makes the tea,' he said, suddenly releasing her hand, and diving into the waves.

Anna followed. It was only as she neared the shore that she saw someone was standing there. Even before she reached it, she could see his smile.

How long has Ryan been there, she wondered. But as soon as he spoke; she knew.

'So mermaids still try to lure men to their doom,' he said, twisting the towel round her wet body, and with vicious fingers began to rub her dry.

CHAPTER SEVEN

Tears stung Anna's eyes as sand scoured her skin and she wriggled out of Ryan's grasp, clutching the towel round her.

'What are you doing here?' Cameron demanded; frowning at his brother.

Ryan raised one eyebrow.

'Do I need an invitation to visit now?'

Anna could sense the antagonism between them. But why was Cameron so angry? She saw Ryan's lips curve into that mocking smile, a smile that never reached his eyes which remained like cool blue ice.

'Come on, Gran will be waiting,' she reminded them, starting to run up the beach. 'Does she know you're here, Ryan?'

'We've spoken. That's how I knew where to find you. But then, I could've guessed. That rock always held a fascination for you as a child, didn't it, Anna? That and sandcastles, and fires.'

Her chin jutted and she tried to outpace him, but soon realised it was impossible.

Gran was sitting at the table when they entered the kitchen, hands clasped round a mug. Lines of tiredness were etched deep into her cheeks and, despite her tan, she looked pale.

She's getting old, Anna thought, and

sadness swept over her.

'Out of those wet things before you flood the room,' she chided.

Anna couldn't help smiling. Yet another of those old, familiar phrases. Having the twins here again brought them all back. Two at a time, she leaped up the stairs and was in the bathroom before Cameron could reach it first.

Memories of their shared moments, out on the rock, filled her mind as the warm water streamed over her. It was the first time Cameron had kissed her, almost the first time anyone had ever kissed her, really kissed her, that is. She'd always been much too aware of the scar on her cheek to let anyone come close.

She stepped from the shower and with one hand wiped away steam clouding the mirror. Then, holding her long dark hair away from her face, she leaned forward, turning her head sideways. Lightly, her questing fingers touched the skin. To her, its unnatural texture was so obvious. Yet Cameron hadn't appeared to notice as his lips feathered across her skin.

Letting her hair fall back, she quickly pulled on her clothes and undid the bathroom door, to find Cameron waiting patiently.

'Sorry about all the sand,' she said, with a grin. 'I decided it wasn't worth cleaning it up, when you're only going to add to it.'

As she went downstairs, she could hear the rise and fall of Ryan's and Gran's voices which ceased when she went into the kitchen. Her grandmother was tight-lipped and a faint flush of colour tinged her cheek-bones. Anna wondered just what Ryan had been saying and why he was here at all.

'Won't Laura be expecting you back?' she asked, opening the fridge and taking out lettuce, cucumber and tomatoes.

'I don't live in her pocket, Anna. Besides, I thought it would be pleasant to stop over and catch up on news with you and Gran.'

Anna met his gaze.

'Strange you haven't done so for the last six years, Ryan.'

His smile was back.

'And now I want to make amends. Can we forget all that happened and start afresh? My grandfather's death was a distressing time for everyone, I know, most of all for me. We were very close.'

'Until Anna came,' Cameron said, coming through the door, buttoning his shirt. 'After that, Grandpa was fully aware of how you tormented her.'

'Tormented her! Anna, tell him that's not true. Teased her, yes. Nothing more.'

'Stop arguing, boys, and sit down at the table. Cameron will you carve the ham? Ryan, you can open a bottle of wine. White, I think. Anna, that salad will drown if you keep on washing it. For goodness' sake, put it in the bowl.'

It's just as though we were children again, with Gran giving out orders, Anna thought, slicing tomatoes over the lettuce, and adding chunks of cucumber.

'So what are you doing here?' Cameron asked his brother.

'He wants me to let him have Trevellion Farm,' Sally said abruptly, spooning vinaigrette into one of Anna's little glazed jugs.

Anna put the bowl of salad in the centre of the table.

'Don't you think you ought to explain why you can't, Gran?'

Ryan looked up from uncorking the bottle.

'Explain what? My company is prepared to make a very good offer. What use is a derelict, old farm to you? This house will last you for the rest of your days.'

'So it is you behind the caravan scheme,' Cameron roared. 'I guessed as much.'

'Boys!'

Sally's tone brought silence.

'I'm afraid you're too late, Ryan. Trevellion Farm belongs to Cameron.'

'But you outbid him.'

'All I've done is loan him fifty thousand pounds. The rest of the money was Cameron's. And before you say or do anything else, Ryan, it's all been sighed and sealed legally.'

Anna couldn't believe that Ryan was smiling again.

'Well, then, Gran, I shall have to give in with

73

good grace, won't I? Can't bear a bad loser. I see the bunk beds are still in our old room, so you won't mind if I stay overnight, will you?'

He drained his glass and refilled it.

'I never drink and drive.'

Anna felt a sense of foreboding all through their meal. Ryan was behaving in such a charming manner. Somehow it didn't seem quite right. Ryan wasn't like that, never had been. If anything didn't go how he wanted it, there was always trouble.

Surely he can't have changed completely over the years, she thought, watching him across the table.

As if reading what was in her mind, he raised his glass and smiled. It sent a shiver quivering down the length of her spine and she wished he wasn't staying the night.

Cameron was very quiet. Overshadowed by his brother, Anna decided. That hadn't changed. Whenever Ryan wasn't around, Cameron had always been so different, but once his twin returned . . .

The wine was making her sleepy. Her head felt heavy, making it difficult to concentrate. She closed her eyes and felt herself begin to drift. Around her she could hear the murmur of the others' conversation, but not their words.

'Anna, darling, wake up.'

Gran was shaking her shoulder.

'You've been asleep for hours. We're all

74

going to bed now. I think you'd better do the same.'

Once there, however, she didn't feel tired any more. She could smell the salt of the sea through the open window, hear waves pound the rocks down in the cove. High tide, she thought. The wind always gets stronger then.

From the room next door came the creak of a bunk bed as one of the twins climbed in. It was a sound she'd heard so many times in the past. Was it Cameron or Ryan? Why has Ryan decided to stay, she wondered again.

For six years I haven't seen or heard from either of the twins and now they're both here again. Everyone together.

The last time was when . . .

She pushed the memory from her mind, but it kept edging back. It had been the night of the fire. Even with her eyes tight closed she could still picture it—the flames, the open doorway, Tom silhouetted there.

Her teeth bit down into her lip and she tasted blood.

Why did we have that party, she asked herself.

Ryan's face floated into her vision, the way he was smiling, and that girl, together in the darkness, lit only by the flicker of lightning. Then she was running back through the garden, feeling the first heavy drops of rain, hearing the thunder, seeing the outline of the shed, then feeling the softness and warmth of the cushions.

Her head sank deeper into the pillow, remembering.

The smell of smoke woke her. At first she was sure it was part of her dream, until she began to cough. Somewhere, near her room, was a sound she recognised, a crackle that seemed to grow into a roar, and reflected on the panes of the open window she could see the flames.

Throwing back the duvet, she grabbed her dressing-gown and ran to the door, turning the handle, tugging at it. It refused to open. She felt for the key. The lock was empty. Any minute now the floorboards would start to blacken, then flames creep up through, twisting, curling, growing higher. Her fists banged frantically on the door, her voice screaming out.

'Help!'

Tears welled behind her eyes, then brimmed over. A faint click made her take hold of the door handle again, twisting it in desperation. This time it turned and she was out on the landing, gasping for air. Arms caught her as she fell. Ryan or Cameron? She wasn't sure, her eyes blurred by tears and smoke.

'Downstairs quickly.'

Still she couldn't tell.

'Through the front door. The studio's on fire.'

'Oh, Anna! You're safe!'

Gran was holding her now. Bewildered, Anna clung on, face buried in her grandmother's quilted shoulder. In the distance she could hear the wail of sirens. Headlights wavered along the lane, dazzling as they came up the drive and a fire engine braked to a halt.

Soon water jetted into the air, sending up a shower of spray as it met the walls. A spotlight illuminated the area, revealing dark figures moving, hoses snaking across the gravel. Then more sirens, more vehicles crunching up the drive. To Anna it was all so familiar. Cameron! Where was Cameron? And Ryan, too.

Someone was wrapping a blanket round her shaking body, guiding her towards the open doors at the back of an ambulance.

'No,' she protested, struggling.

'It's all right, love. Just need to check you out.'

Still protesting, she was half-carried inside, laid on a bed, and a mask was pressed over her nose and mouth. Her throat choked, then eased as she breathed in coolness.

The ambulance began to move. Anna tore off the mask, raising her head. 'Cameron. Where's Cameron?'

'It's all right, darling.'

Anna sank back. Gran's voice! Calm, reassuring.

'The boys are fine. They've stayed behind to keep an eye on things. It's only the studio.'

'But how?' Anna croaked through dry lips.

Her grandmother shrugged.

'Who knows? Possibly the kiln overheated. You were working there earlier today, weren't you? Was it switched on?'

Anna tried to think back. She'd been on the wheel when she'd heard Cameron arrive. They'd left then, to go swimming. Then Ryan had appeared.

They'd eaten their meal, and she'd never returned to the studio. But had the kiln been switched on? Anna couldn't remember.

It was late the following afternoon when Anna came home again. Her throat and chest still ached from the smoke. Cameron drove Gran over to Truro to collect her from the hospital.

'The studio,' she wanted to know. 'Is there much damage?'

'Not too bad,' Cameron reassured her.

But when she saw it, she was horrified. Every window frame was burned, glass lying on the floor, shattered by the heat. Every wooden shelf and every mug, vase, jug, bowl, cup and saucer on them, every cupboard, and the long, wooden bench she worked at, totally destroyed. All that remained was a shell of blackened walls.

Her only consolation was that she'd delivered most of her orders during the week, and the bowls she'd been working on were a batch scheduled for ten days' time.

'Don't worry, darling,' her grandmother said. 'No-one was hurt. None of this matters. It can be replaced. People can't.'

Ryan was still there when she arrived. She wondered why. He came to stand behind her as she examined the ruins.

'Strange, how fire seems to follow you, Anna,' he murmured, his mouth brushing her cheek as he leaned close to her ear.

She turned to face him.

'And only when you're around, Ryan.'

'And Cameron,' he said, smiling. 'Cameron's always there, too. You hadn't thought of that, had you?'

His words jolted through her.

On the landing, outside her bedroom door that night, which of them had it been? And the key. She was quite sure the key wasn't there and the door was locked. But why? Was it to scare her?

The studio was built on to the side of the house, below her bedroom. A fire there would take time to reach her, just enough time for her to escape. But if the door was locked . . .

It had to be an accident.

The fire in the shed all these years ago— that was an accident. No-one had proved it to be otherwise. This had to be an accident also.

CHAPTER EIGHT

While the studio was being completely renovated, planning permission was granted to adapt it for use as a shop, something that raised a few eyebrows among the gossips in the village, who regarded the fire as being rather convenient.

With new orders to complete, Anna had to work in the kitchen for the next few weeks and this slowed her down considerably. At the same time, Cameron was over at Trevellion Farm, supervising the careful reconstruction there.

The summer was turning very hot and with the good weather came hordes of tourists, filling the beaches and crowding every narrow lane with their cars. Unless Anna went very early in the morning, swimming in the cove was almost impossible. Anna and Sally, and Cameron when he was staying, tried to go down there well before breakfast, but even at that hour the windsurfers were often ahead of them.

'I'm dreading that wedding next weekend,' Anna confided to Cameron when, for once, they had the cove to themselves and had swum out to the rock.

'You're dreading it! What about me? I'm the best man, don't forget.'

Anna traced a bead of water meandering down his back with her finger.

'I wish we didn't have to stay there though.'

'Just think of it as three days wallowing in the lap of luxury, and enjoy the time there. Our wedding won't be a bit like this, I promise.'

She jerked upright.

'What did you say?'

Cameron's blue eyes were laughing down at her.

'I said, our wedding won't be a bit like this.'

'Is that a proposal?' Anna asked in astonishment.

'Do you really need one? I thought my intentions were pretty obvious. Anyway, this rock's a bit hard to go down on one knee and I'll probably slide off.'

'Are you quite sure you want to marry me? It's not just because Ryan . . .'

'No, it is not! I love you, Anna. I always have and I always will, ever since that first day when you came to stay here. You were such a lost and lonely little girl.'

'But you didn't contact me for all those years,' she protested.

'I know, but I didn't stop loving you. After what happened the night of the fire, I just thought that Ryan and I would be a constant reminder.'

She put her hand to the side of her face.

'This is the constant reminder, Cameron,

and I'll never be able to escape from that.'

Lifting away her hair, his fingers touched the scar, and then he kissed her cheek.

'Why do you let it worry you so much, Anna? It's hardly noticeable.'

'Except to me. I'm branded with the death of your grandfather. Surely every time you look at me, you must be reminded, too.'

'When I look at you, Anna, all I see is the woman I love, and have always loved. Nothing else. My grandfather gave his life to save yours. He loved you very much, Anna. And if it had been you who died in that fire, and he'd lived, he would never have recovered or forgiven himself.'

'Does Ryan feel the same?' she asked, her gaze searching his.

'Even I don't know my brother well enough to say.'

He caught her hand and pulled her to her feet.

'Come on, it's breakfast time. Don't forget, last one to the beach makes the tea!'

The following weekend, with their wedding clothes carefully packed in the car boot, Cameron drove Anna and Sally to Laura's ancestral home.

'The estate starts here,' he told them, as the road ran along beside a high, granite wall for a mile or so, until they came to a gatehouse that arched over studded, wooden doors.

An elderly man hobbled out, asked for their

names, then consulted a typed list, before letting the car through.

'It's huge!' Anna breathed, staring at the building.

Cameron grinned.

'Only eighty-one rooms, forty-four of which are bedrooms.'

'You're joking!'

He shook his head.

'If you ask nicely, maybe they'll take you on the conducted tour. The house is open to the public three times a week from Easter until the end of October at five pounds a head.'

'And this is where Ryan and Laura are going to live after the wedding?' Sally asked, stepping out from the back seat.

'Yes,' Cameron replied, helping her. 'One of the wings of the house has been modernised for them.'

'Trust Ryan to fall on his feet,' Sally replied drily. 'Shouldn't some servant rush out to usher us inside?'

Even as she asked the question, a dark-suited man came through the door and descended the steps. He bowed from the waist.

'Ladies, sir, good afternoon. I trust you've had a pleasant journey. If you give me your key, sir, I'll ask one of the chauffeurs to unload your car, then garage it.'

'Note, one of the chauffeurs,' Sally whispered in Anna's ear. 'Is this the butler, do you think?'

'If you would follow me, I'll take you inside. The housekeeper will show you to your rooms and tea will be waiting in the drawing-room when you are ready.'

Subdued, Anna and Sally followed behind him, through an entrance porch and thick, wooden door into what Anna could only guess was the original Great Hall. Panelled in oak, the high room had an enormous fireplace on one wall, with a large, gilt-framed portrait over it. There was no mistaking the painting. Dressed in a deep turquoise-blue velvet dress that revealed creamy-white shoulders and tiny waist before it flowed down in heavy folds to the ground, Laura reclined—Anna could think of no other suitable word for it—on a gold silk-covered sofa.

Her auburn hair was swept up, away from her delicate features, and clung in a festoon of curls at the back of her head. It was the first thing anyone saw on entering the room.

No wonder Ryan fell in love with her, Anna thought, stifling a twinge of what she knew could only be jealousy.

'This way, please.'

A matronly woman in a black dress and lace-edged white apron ushered them out through another door, along a carpeted corridor to the foot of a curving staircase that seemed to hang suspended in air.

'Cantilevered,' Cameron whispered, seeing Anna's doubtful expression. 'Don't worry, It's quite safe.'

Another long corridor led from the top of the stairs, bordered by doors on either side. At one the housekeeper stopped and opened it.

'Miss Penryn?'

She looked from Sally to Anna.

'This is your room, madam. I hope you'll find everything to your satisfaction. There's a telephone beside the bed, if you should require anything. Tea is being served in the drawing-room.'

Inside the room, Anna tried not to laugh. It was all so unbelievable. Butlers, chauffeurs, housekeeper, all in formal uniform. It was like stepping back in time. Her suitcase, she noticed, was already in the room. There must be back stairs, because no member of staff had passed them on their journey.

She gazed round. A four-poster bed, hung with red velvet and gold tassels, dominated the room. The furniture was old and ornate—matching velvet-covered chairs and a sofa; wardrobe; chest of drawers and dressing-table in a highly-polished rich dark wood.

She opened a door half-hidden in the panelling to reveal a bathroom, but this was completely modern, with shower and toilet. Thick cream towels hung on a heated rail. The walls were mirrored and a selection of bath oils, creams and talcum powder were arranged on a glass shelf.

After her grandmother's tiny, old-fashioned

bathroom, this was sheer luxury.

Tea was being served in the drawing-room, she remembered. Quickly washing her hands and brushing her dark hair over her cheek, Anna opened the bedroom door.

Now where do I go, she asked herself. Maybe we should have been issued with the official guidebook.

'Lost, Anna?'

A hand caught her elbow, spinning her round. Ryan was smiling; at her.

'The drawing-room,' Anna said, trying unsuccessfully to pull away. 'The housekeeper told us tea was being served there.'

'Mrs Treloar, you mean. Come on then. I'll show you.'

His grip tightened, thumb digging into the muscles of her arm.

'No more fires, I hope?'

Almost running to keep up with his fast pace, she ignored the mocking question, hoping he would slow down before they descended the stairs.

'Did you know this place is haunted?' he said, stopping in front of a gilt-framed portrait on the landing. 'Probably by her. Beautiful, isn't she?'

Anna studied the painting. Dark brown eyes fringed with thick lashes gazed back, full of provocation. Black hair, caught to one side, cascaded over bare shoulders on to a full, almost visible, bosom. Red lips, slightly parted,

86

revealed even white teeth.

'Who was she?' Anna asked.

'Laura's great-great, and probably a few more greats, grandmother, also a Laura. Quite a naughty lady, from all accounts. Pity her namesake doesn't take after her.'

'And she's supposed to haunt the house?' Ryan laughed.

'Oh, yes. Came to rather a nasty end. Husband caught her, snuggled up in a four-poster with one of her many lovers. Single sword thrust went through the pair of them.'

Anna shuddered, and exclaimed, 'Ugh! How horrible!'

'Some nights, if you listen carefully, you can hear the rustle of her silk skirts as she walks along the corridors.'

'Have you heard anything?' Anna asked, deciding that Ryan was now inventing the story.

His mouth curved.

'Not yet.'

'Ah, there you are.'

Sally came along the corridor towards them.

'Thank goodness for that. I'm dying for a cup of tea. On you go, Ryan. At least you know the way.'

Holding her grandmother's arm, Anna walked down the stairs beside her, thankful that Ryan went ahead. When he opened the drawing-room door, she could only gasp at the splendour of it.

The ceiling was pale blue and lavishly gilded, the walls almost hidden by paintings and more gilding. An unbelievable amount of beautiful furniture, including a grand piano, scarcely filled any of the space and the polished, wooden floor was covered with elaborately-patterned carpets backed in deep red. Another huge fireplace dominated one wall, with a coat of arms above it.

Several people were scattered around the room, sitting on gold brocade sofas or lost in deep chairs. Among them Anna was relieved to see Cameron, who stood up and came across to meet them.

'Wait!' Ryan said, glowering at his brother. 'They haven't been introduced to Laura's parents yet.'

Slipping an arm through each of theirs, he led the way to where a couple were seated, deep in conversation with, Anna guessed from his clothes, the vicar. All glanced up as Ryan reached them, and both men rose to their feet.

'Molly, Frank, this is Sally Delabole, my step-grandmother, and Anna Penryn, her granddaughter.'

Anna found her hand lost in the roughened one of Laura's father who, in tweed jacket and expensive-looking fawn trousers, towered above her.

'Ah!' he boomed. 'The gel who was saved from the fire.'

It was one of those moments of complete

silence that occurs sometimes in a room full of conversation. Anna's body tensed, and she was conscious of everyone looking at her.

'Not once, but twice, Frank,' Ryan observed, and his smile made Anna's skin prickle as he swept back her hair. 'See the scars?'

'You poor child. How simply awful for you.'

Laura's mother gripped her hand and gave it a squeeze. Her eyes, Anna saw, were full of genuine sympathy.

'Here, take my tea. I haven't drunk any yet.'

Cameron was at her side, holding out a cup.

'There's a seat over by the window.'

Firmly, he steered her through the crush of people and sat down next to her.

'One day I'll wring my brother's neck,' he murmured through clenched teeth. 'Are you OK?'

A tiny smile quivered on her lips. Once again Cameron was asking that question. He raised one eyebrow.

'What have I said that's so funny?'

'You always seem to be asking if I'm all right,' she said.

'Maybe because I'm always having to rescue you from Ryan.'

She sipped the tea.

'Oh, lovely. Earl Grey.'

'What else would you expect in these surroundings? It's quite a place, isn't it? Stay there and I'll go and find you something to eat.'

Anna watched him weave through the chattering groups, seeing his dark head reach the far side of the room, disappear, then reappear as he made the journey back again.

'I hope dinner will be a substantial one,' he said ruefully, handing her a plate with two tiny triangular cucumber sandwiches, two miniature meringues and two chocolate fingers on it. 'Good job we stopped for lunch on the way.'

She took one of the sandwiches.

'Where's Laura? I thought she'd be here to welcome everyone.'

'Getting ready, I suppose. There's a rehearsal for tomorrow at the church in half an hour. I've had my orders. That's why the vicar's here.'

Dinner was indeed more substantial, and took over three hours! Anna lost count of the number of courses and different wines that appeared. By eleven o'clock, when they'd at last reached the coffee stage, she was trying desperately not to yawn.

'Anna, my dear, I won't take no for an answer. You must have a liqueur,' Laura's father bellowed down the table, after she'd declined. 'Sleep like a top, you will then.'

Smiling, Ryan leaned towards her from the opposite side.

'And not notice any ghostly manifestations.'

Reluctantly, she sipped a glass of liqueur, feeling the burn of the liquid scald her throat.

'I really must go to bed,' she said, resting her head against Cameron's shoulder and yawning again. 'I'll nod off here if I don't. Gran went up ages ago.'

'Come on then, I'll take you.'

Puffing at a cigar, Ryan tipped back in his chair.

'Don't forget your room is at the opposite end of the house, little brother, will you? Safety precaution. So we know where everyone is.'

His eyes slanted towards Anna.

'In case of fire.'

She stood up, gripping the edge of the table to keep her balance, seeing that slow smile creep across his face.

With Cameron's arm round her, together they climbed the stairs and stopped outside her bedroom door.

'Are you . . .' He paused.

She laughed and reached up to slip her arms round his neck as she kissed him.

'All right? Yes, Cameron. I'm fine. Slightly tipsy, but fine.'

CHAPTER NINE

It was a perfect day for a wedding. Sun not too hot, clear blue sky, and in such a lovely setting. The guests all made their own way across to the church. It was only a short walk away, in the grounds.

'Every member of the family's been christened, married and buried here for centuries,' Laura's father had told them in great detail over dinner the previous evening.

Inside, the church was cool. Posies of white flowers hung from the end of every pew, scenting the air with a heavy perfume. Ryan and Cameron were already waiting.

Anna thought how handsome they looked in their formal dark jackets and grey trousers. Only their gold silk waistcoats and cravats provided colour. Subdued voices murmured. Elaborate hats swayed as heads twisted to view each new arrival. Hymn sheets rustled. Anna looked at her watch.

'She's very late,' she whispered to her grandmother.

'A bride should be. I kept Tom waiting for nearly half an hour. He thought I'd changed my mind. Traffic jam actually. A broken-down coach was blocking the lane.'

Ryan seemed unperturbed. It was Cameron who kept turning round. Anna could see anxiety sharpen his face.

I won't keep him waiting at our wedding, she thought.

Then with a sudden roar of sound, the organ bellowed into life. Under her high-heeled shoes, Anna felt the stone floor tremble.

In a swathe of veiling and rustling silk, Laura drifted down the aisle, her hand resting lightly on her father's arm. Behind her came a procession of ten bridesmaids, ranging in height from tiny to adult, either side of her long train. All were dressed in gold silk, matching the men's waistcoats.

Is it to signify the family's wealth, or just that Laura likes the colour, Anna wondered.

A trailing bouquet of white lilies was handed to the smallest bridesmaid, who spent the rest of the ceremony sitting on the floor, head bent over it. When she stood up at the end, no-one realised she'd been carefully removing the petals until they scattered in a waxy shower round her!

Anna gazed at the memorials inscribed on the church walls—Laura's ancestors. She wondered which of them was for the other Laura, whose portrait hung on the landing, above the stairs.

A choirboy sang a psalm while the register was being signed in the vestry. His clear, high voice rose up to the rafters and echoed, every word like the delicate notes of a bell. Then the organ was thundering out the Wedding March and Ryan and his bride reappeared, to walk down the aisle.

Anna forced herself to look at them, and discovered Ryan's blue eyes staring back at her. As they passed, his head turned slightly and his mouth curved into a smile that made her shiver. Why did he always have that disturbing effect on her?

Behind them, Cameron's expression was still worried. Taking his duties as best man so seriously, Anna thought. And the worst is yet to come for him—making a speech. She wished she could be there, next to him, instead of the tall, elegant bridesmaid who looked as though she'd stepped off the cover of a glossy magazine.

Bending her head forward, she shook her hair round her cheek and joined the procession leaving the church.

The reception seemed to go on for ever. First, the meal—a buffet such as Anna had never seen before—in the Great Hall. Anna decided the staff must have been up all night, decorating the huge room with floral arrangements. They were far too grand to be called vases of flowers.

She couldn't guess how many guests were there, several hundred at least. The room was crammed with people and, with glasses and plates balanced in their hands, they spilled out on to the lawns.

It couldn't be a more glorious day, Anna thought, perching herself on a low, stone wall overlooking a series of rose beds. She'd left her grandmother, deep in conversation with a couple who were also artists, whom she'd met before.

The bridal pair were circulating together among their guests and, seeing them coming near, Anna had escaped into the garden. No way could she face Ryan, or Laura.

Cameron's speech had gone down surprisingly well. He'd related the usual anecdotes about life with his twin, toasted the bridesmaids, and looked startled by the burst of enthusiastic applause at the end. The last Anna had seen of him was with the smallest bridesmaid clinging to the tails of his jacket and refusing to be separated. Anna decided the little girl had taken her duty of holding the bride's train very seriously, and now clung on to anything that trailed.

From where she sat, Anna could look down on the estuary where the sun was disappearing in a final glow of colour, sending long fingers of scarlet and orange shimmering over the water.

Like flames, she thought, and her heart thudded.

It was growing chilly in the garden now. People were beginning to move towards the house. Inside, she could see lights appearing in different rooms. Soon, dancing was to begin.

Laura and Ryan were leaving for their honeymoon the following morning. Anna hoped she could avoid coming into contact with Ryan until they'd gone.

After today, she need never see him again, listen to his taunting remarks and no longer be aware of his eyes always on her—or was it her imagination?

A hand touched her shoulder and she jumped, the empty plate slipping off her lap on to the grass. In the shadowy twilight, she couldn't tell whether it was Ryan or Cameron who stood there. Dressed in the same formal suits, they looked identical.

'Are you OK? It's getting cold.'

Her body relaxed.

'Cameron,' she said, raising her face to his kiss.

'Come back indoors, Anna. There's no need to hide out here. The dancing's started and I need a partner.'

'What about your little companion?'

She felt his mouth smile against her cheek.

'Been dragged, screaming loudly, off to bed.'

He tugged at his jacket.

'The tails of this will never be the same again. She's been using them as a serviette.'

With arms round each other's waists, they walked back across the lawn. A wave of music and voices, mingled with heat and vying perfumes, met them as they went in through the open doors. Firmly, Cameron guided her into the mass of swaying bodies.

The heat and the noise and the wine gave Anna a throbbing headache as the evening progressed.

'Have you any painkillers?' she whispered, finding her grandmother on one of the sofas in the drawing-room, chatting to some of the older guests who'd retired there for quietness.

'In my bedroom, darling, on the dressing-table. Do you want me to come up with you?'

Anna shook her head.

'I'll find them.'

'Is Cameron with you?'

'No, he's gone to organise drinks for the musicians, Gran.'

Walking slowly so as not to jolt her head too much, Anna climbed the stairs. At the top, she paused under the portrait of the first Laura, admiring the sultry provocativeness of her beauty. Was the artist also one of her lovers, Anna wondered. Did that account for such a look?

It was quiet on the landing. Far away, down in the Great Hall, she could hear the music. No disco or band for this wedding, but a quintet of two violins, a cello, saxophone and piano, more suited to a concert platform.

Anna tried to remember which of the many rooms was her grandmother's. It wasn't even in the same corridor as hers. How many bedrooms did Cameron say there were?

Forty-four?

She was quite lost now. Every corridor looked the same, and she'd passed her own room twice already. At the far end, one door was partly open and when she came to it, she heard someone crying.

Anna paused, uncertain whether to go in or not. Cautiously, she pushed the door wider.

Laura, still in her wedding dress, sat hunched on the bed, another four-poster, lavishly draped in white lace and satin. The marriage bed, Anna decided, and wondered how many brides had slept in it before.

Raising her head, mascara smudged and streaked, lipstick gone, leaving a pale mouth, untidy curls of auburn hair clinging to wet cheeks, Laura looked at Anna and her expression wasn't friendly.

'I'm sorry, Laura,' Anna said, hesitantly, 'but I couldn't help hearing . . . Are you all right?'

The other girl's chin lifted, but then quivered and she began to sob, her whole body shaking.

'Oh, Laura.'

Anna sat on the bed beside her, not knowing whether to put her arm round her or not.

'What's wrong? It's your wedding day. You shouldn't be like this.'

'How can you, of all people, ask me that?'

The words were muffled in Laura's hands.

Anna frowned.

'What do you mean?'

'You and Ryan.'

Tensing, Anna sat up straight. Laura's smudged eyes were glaring at her. 'He told me, just now, while we were dancing. He told me he'd been with you last night.'

The silk of her wedding dress twisted between her fingers.

'He loves you, Anna, and he's married me, not because he loves me, but because of my family, my position, and most of all because of my money.'

Anna caught the girl's agitated fingers in hers.

'It's not true, Laura. Ryan hates me. He always has. Right from when I was a child. And, after what happened to his grandfather, he hates me even more. And he's lying about last night. I don't know what he's up to, but he was nowhere near me last night, other than to say a few words before we went to bed.'

Laura's eyes were still full of suspicion.

'Why would he say that to me then?'

'I don't know, Laura. To embarrass me perhaps? Or because Cameron and I are in love, and he can't bear his brother to have anything he can't possess himself. I just don't know.'

She squeezed Laura's hands.

'But believe me, nothing happened last night. I was sound asleep, alone, all night.

99

Nothing happened.'

She could see Laura was unconvinced.

'I've noticed that he never stops looking at you, Anna, or talking about you when we're together.'

'Please, believe me, Laura. Ryan hates me.'

But doubt was settling in her mind, too.

'I want to believe you, Anna. I really do. But . . .'

'Laura, Cameron and I are getting married. We're very much in love. Once we've gone home, Ryan will forget about us again, and you'll be alone together. Now, clean your face and put on some more make-up. Everyone will be wondering what's happened to you.'

With a rather wan smile, Laura went to the dressing-table and began to dab at her face with a tissue.

'Thanks, Anna.'

'I'm just off to find some painkillers. Do you know which is my grandmother's room? I'm completely lost.'

'It's just round the corner, in the next corridor. It's the nearest bedroom this end.'

Closing the door, Anna left her, and continued walking. In Sally's room, she found the tablets, dissolved a couple in a glass of water, and drank them down. The clothes Gran had taken off to dress for the wedding were strewn all over her bed. Anna picked them up and hung them in the wardrobe. By the time she came upstairs, her grandmother would be too tired to tidy them away herself.

Anna's headache began to ease, the tablets rapidly taking effect. She rested her head against the cool glass of the window, gazing out into the garden, illuminated by subdued lamps in trees and under shrubs. Couples appeared and disappeared among the shadows. Beyond, in the estuary, were pinpoints of light twinkling in the distance. The scent of lavender and roses drifted through the open window, soothing, restful. With closed eyes, she breathed it.

Her headache had almost gone. She felt she could face the party again. All she had to do was find her way back along the corridors, wishing they were not quite so dark. At last, recognising the painting of that other Laura, she knew where she was. The stairs were just ahead. Behind her, Anna thought she heard a movement. Swiftly, she turned. No-one, yet she was sure someone was there. The back of her neck prickled.

What was it Ryan had said? At times, you could hear the rustle of Laura's silk skirts as her ghost walked along the landing. A wisp of smoke coiled towards her. Anna's eyes widened. Smoke! She stepped backwards, away from it. Fingers suddenly dug into her shoulders, twisting her round. She opened her mouth to scream.

Then she was falling, hitting something hard, bouncing off it and continuing to fall, pain shooting through her body, until she came to rest in a heap at the bottom of the staircase. In a confusion of noise and movement, the smell of smoke was growing stronger. Then came the sound she knew so well—the crackle and roar of flames.

Another fire! Darkness whirled and spun her down into a vortex from which Anna couldn't escape . . .

She was lying on one of the gold sofas when she opened her eyes. Cameron and her grandmother, their faces both as anxious as each other, gazed down at her.

'Oh, Anna, are you . . .'

Her mouth twitched painfully, and she whispered, 'Yes, Cameron, I'm fine.'

She tried to sit up, but sank back again, her head throbbing.

'What happened?'

'A fire, Anna. I'm afraid Laura is . . .'

Anna closed her eyes, tears weeping through their lids. She didn't need to be told. It had happened again. Another fire—and this time Laura was the innocent victim.

'How?'

She had to ask, had to know.

'Somehow the bed . . .'

'All that lace,' Anna murmured.

Cameron stared at her.

'You've seen it?'

Anna nodded.

'I was there, talking to Laura. She was

upset.'

Ryan's face loomed over her.

'You were in that room, with Laura?'

His nails dug down into her shoulders, shaking her.

'Why, Anna? Laura was my wife. Were you so jealous you had to kill her, like you killed my grandfather?'

'Leave her alone!'

Cameron reached out, trying to hold his brother back.

'Murderer!'

Leaning forward, Ryan spat out the word, but even as she stared back at him, Anna saw his mouth curl into a twisted smile.

CHAPTER TEN

Questions, questions, and more questions. It was just like before. Anna's head ached. Her body ached, too. She didn't want to answer any more questions, but they were relentless.

Ryan had accused her. Everyone there had heard him. The police had no option but to question her. She was the last person to see Laura alive.

'Except her killer,' Anna said.

Her clothes were taken away and examined. Nothing was found on them, or her skin; no trace of her having started a fire. It could only have been an accident, Laura maybe smoking a cigarette? Everyone knew she did, especially when stressed.

Was she smoking when I was talking to her, Anna asked herself, but couldn't remember.

Cameron, Sally and Anna stayed on. While the police enquiry was taking place, they had no choice. It was an uncomfortable situation. After his initial outburst, Ryan calmed down, even apologised to Anna. It worried her, as it was so unlike Ryan.

Eventually, the questions ceased and everyone was allowed to return home. In their absence, work on the studio-shop continued. Now it was almost complete, and Anna was delighted.

She had a great deal to catch up on. With the summer season well underway, local pottery was in great demand from tourists who wanted a memento of their holiday.

Cameron, too, was busy over at Trevellion Farm. Anna joined him there one evening and together they toured the house.

'I was right, you know,' he said quietly. 'The original building was definitely Elizabethan. Just look at that fireplace now. And upstairs, come and see the ceiling.'

Taking her hand, he led the way, and once inside the room, she looked up, amazed. The low ceiling had been removed, revealing another of ornate plaster, depicting scenes from the Bible.

'There's a similar one in the library of Lanhydrock, a National Trust house near Bodmin,' Cameron told her. 'Much larger, but this could have been done by the same craftsman, probably in the mid-sixteen-hundreds.'

In another week, the shop would officially be open. If the autumn weather turned out to be as good as the summer, it would extend the season and also their trade.

Anna worked all hours, producing the long vases that had once been Tom's speciality, having finally mastered the technique, as well as the popular named mugs and her own little models of Cornish properties.

Her grandmother, too, had been busy and

her evenings were spent, with Cameron's help, framing the water colours she painted during the day. Everything seemed to be turning out well, at last—then came the news that Laura's body had been released and her funeral now could take place.

A personal note from Ryan begged them to attend. Cameron explained that their parents were again abroad and unable to be there.

'We can't refuse then, can we, Gran?' Anna said. 'We are the only family he has.'

The car journey there brought back all the memories. Before, for the wedding, they'd been reluctant to go. This time it was even worse. Anna wasn't sure what kind of reception she'd receive. She seemed to leave the damage of a fire behind her, wherever she went.

Once again, they were to stay overnight.

Laura's portrait still dominated the Great Hall, but this time it was wreathed in swathes of black ribbon. Everywhere, Anna noticed, was similarly adorned. Where once there'd been huge bowls of flowers, now there were white lilies. The smell of them hung heavily in the air, cloying.

The funeral was to be early the following morning.

'Laura adored being out riding before the dew was gone,' her mother said, her voice choked with emotion. 'Her horse—Daybreak —will be part of the cortège to the church, of course.'

Horses were a major part of the procession making its way to the little church that morning. The glass-sided carriage bearing Laura's coffin was drawn by four of them, black plumes tossing on their heads. Behind trotted a white mare, saddled as if ready for its rider.

It's all so different from the day we last made this journey to the church, Anna thought, walking slowly beside her grandmother, everyone so solemn and silent.

Ryan and Cameron were together, directly behind Laura's parents. Anna wished that Cameron was with her. She needed his comfort.

Here, she was among the same people who'd been at the wedding and some, she was sure, were doubtful about her part in Laura's death. She'd hardly slept the previous night, scared that Ryan might appear. When dawn finally inched into the dark sky, she dozed for a while, but was woken by the breakfast gong at seven-thirty.

At nine o'clock, when the clock in the stable-yard began to strike, the funeral procession set off.

As they filed through the low arch of the church door into musty gloom, Ryan caught Anna's elbow and pulled her close to the wall.

His voice was husky, his lips brushing her ear, as he whispered, 'I want you to marry me, Anna.'

Mourners coming through the door swept her along with them. She tried to turn back, but Ryan was already lost in a crush of people. All she could do was look at him, across the aisle, her mind churning. How could Ryan ask this? Ryan, who hated her so much.

But does he hate me, she puzzled. Laura said he never stopped talking about me. What, though, did he say? Do I love him? As a child it was Ryan's approval I always wanted. Cameron's I knew I already had.

She looked across at the two brothers, so alike, but so different. Which of them do I really love, she wondered as the service began.

*   *   *

There was a buffet lunch after the ceremony.

'The traditional funereal baked meats,' Sally murmured, taking a plate and helping herself to a thick slice of home-baked ham and spooning on different salads.

Below Laura's portrait in the Great Hall, sheaths of white lilies were placed. Like a shrine, Anna thought, looking up at the painting. She really was beautiful . . .that creamy complexion, that lovely auburn hair. No-one will forget her beauty. It's recorded here for ever.

Anna's fingers touched the puckered skin of her cheek and she turned away to see Ryan, on the other side of the room, watching her, a smile hovering faintly around his mouth.

I want you to marry me—the words echoed in her brain.

'Ryan's a very wealthy man now,' Cameron said, following her gaze. Anna bit into a vol-au-vent.

'Is he?' she said, brushing crumbs of pastry from her black skirt.

'All Laura's money will be his. Quite a fortune. She inherited just over a million from her grandmother when she was twenty-one.'

Anna's mind began to whirl. Is it just a coincidence? Everything was following the same pattern? Ryan knew I was to inherit our grandparents' money and if I had died in the shed fire, it would have been his and Cameron's. Now Laura had died in a fire and all her wealth was to pass on to him.

Is it just me this trail of fire follows, or Ryan?

Anna's thoughts flashed back. Everything began that first day on the beach, with Ryan's hand on my back, pushing me down into the flames. She thought about the six years that Ryan and Cameron had been out of her life. What happened then? Neither of them talks about that time. Were there other fires, fires that were assumed to be accidental?

Ryan had reached the top of his professional tree quickly and easily, but how had he got there?

'Anna, are you OK?'

For a moment she looked blankly at Cameron.

'Yes,' she said, and then continued, 'Cameron, when you both left us that summer, after your grandfather died, where did you go?'

His forehead wrinkled.

'Ecuador. It was our gap year before university.'

'Doing what?'

'Clearing areas of jungle. Setting up villages. Why do you want to know, and especially after all this time?'

'Were there ever any fires?'

He laughed.

'What a strange question, Anna. Of course there were. We burned a lot of-the vegetation we cut down.'

'Did anyone die?'

'Well, yes, there was one unfortunate accident, involving the American guy leading our particular group. His sleeping bag caught fire one night. Ryan took his place.'

Her hand shook slightly, spilling the wine she was drinking.

'Ryan did? And after that you both went to university?'

'Yes. Look, Gran's over there. Let's go and join her.'

She caught hold of his arm.

'Not for a minute, Cameron. Tell me more.'

'Why all these questions, Anna?'

'I'm curious, that's all. Did anything happen while you were at university?'

'Oh, Anna! Lots of things happened. Life's like that.'

'How about fires?'

'Why this obsession with fire, Anna?'

'Well, it does seem to follow us around, doesn't it?'

He put his arm round her shoulders and hugged her.

'I'm sorry, Anna. I should have realised. All this must bring back so many memories for you. For goodness' sake, sit down. You're tipping that drink everywhere.'

Balancing his plate on his knee, he sat beside her on one of the gold sofas.

'Come to think of it, there was a fire while we were at university, in one of the halls of residence. Several of the students were injured.'

'Did Ryan benefit in any way?'

He looked sharply at her.

'Benefit? That's a strange thing to say. No, I can't see that he did. One or two of them were taking the same course, I think.'

'And since university?' Anna persisted.

Cameron frowned.

'What is all this about, Anna?'

Putting her empty plate and wine glass on a side table, she caught hold of his hand.

'There have been two tragedies resulting

from fire in our lives, Cameron. All three of us were there at the time.'

'And you think it's Ryan?'

'Or you, or me. I just don't know. Neither time can I remember what happened. I was asleep in the shed, but I've no idea how that fire started, and then when Laura died, someone pushed me down the stairs, knocking me out.'

'Why suspect Ryan and not me?'

His fingers suddenly curled round hers, gripping them tight.

'Or do you suspect me, too, Anna?'

'Laura's death doesn't leave you a fortune, Cameron.'

'I asked if you suspected me, too, Anna. Do you?'

She turned her head away, unable to meet his questioning gaze, and felt his fingers slowly slip away.

CHAPTER ELEVEN

Now that the studio-shop was open, Anna and her grandmother were constantly busy. Seeing them through the bow-fronted window, Anna turning pots on her wheel and Sally quietly painting at her easel, encouraged people to come inside and watch. Once there, they soon found the different crafts on sale irresistible.

With trade booming, other craftsmen were asked to join them, so that customers discovered lace-makers, silversmiths, embroiderers, knitters, wood-carvers or calligraphers to watch while browsing.

Occasionally a coach would make the studio part of its tour and then a sudden surge of tourists crammed the room.

'Next year, we could do coffee and cream teas,' Anna suggested. 'I'm sure there'd be offers of home-made cakes and scones, and plenty of people willing to run it.'

'Darling, we'll be providing the whole village with work soon,' her grandmother said with a smile.

The restoration of Trevellion Farm progressed quite slowly. Skilled work was needed as Cameron kept discovering more and more about the house. After some publicity in the local newspaper, which spread to a wider Press, experts began to visit, eager to contribute their knowledge.

'It'll take a couple of years at least, until it's completed,' Cameron told Anna on one of her rare visits.

'And then what will you do with it?'

Since Laura's funeral, they had drifted apart. Cameron no longer mentioned marriage. It was as though a barrier had grown up between them, something they never talked about.

And all because of my questions, Anna thought.

'Do with it?' he said, and shrugged his shoulders. 'Once, I had plans but now . . . I don't know any more.'

Did those plans include me, she wondered sadly. Was this to have been our home?

Cameron had other projects he was working on, and his visits to Cornwall became less frequent. A foreman was put in charge and the restoration continued.

Of Ryan she heard nothing.

Then it was Sally's eightieth birthday. Anna couldn't believe her grandmother had reached such a wonderful age. She'd always seemed the same, never changing.

Being with her all the time, I suppose I don't notice, Anna thought.

There was to be a party, with all her friends in the village, and Ryan and Cameron. They had to be there. Anna remembered the last party—the twins' eighteenth birthday, so many years ago.

Together, she and her grandmother had designed the party invitations. A printer, one of the craftsmen, produced them, and acceptances came winging back—except from the twins.

Anna couldn't believe they hadn't the courtesy to reply. Both must be working away somewhere, she decided, and the invitations hadn't reached them.

Once more, the party was to be in the cove, but at midday this time. Anna felt a twinge of doubt about the location. Sally was insistent, however. She loved the sea and the beach.

'But, Gran,' Anna said, 'what about the weather?'

'Don't worry, darling. June is always a beautiful month, and for my birthday, it will be perfect.'

She was right. The day dawned clear and warm. For once, the shop was closed. Everyone began to gather on the sand. Some swam, the older ones brought garden chairs and sat in the shade of rocks. Sally greeted them all, beaming.

Anna watched, her eyes slowly filling with tears. Her grandmother's steps were hesitant now and she used a stick to support her. The once-straight back curved. The still wild, uncontrollable hair was pure white as it blew softly round her cheeks.

It seemed no time ago that, regularly, they would both run, hand in hand, across the lane and down on to the beach, into the sea, then they would swim out to their favourite rock.

But it is ages ago now, Anna thought, as her tears brimmed.

'Are you OK?'

She spun round and Cameron caught her, bending to kiss the top of her head.

'Oh, Cameron! I didn't think you'd come.'

'I've been in Tuscany for the last six weeks. A property out there was in need of restoration. I only returned in the early hours of this morning and came straight down. I haven't even been home yet.'

'So you didn't receive the invitation?'

He shook his head.

'I remembered anyway that it was a special birthday for Gran, so here I am. Couldn't miss it, could I?'

'What about Ryan?'

Cameron glanced round.

'Isn't he here?'

'Haven't heard a word since . . .' Anna paused. 'Since the funeral, But I did invite him.'

'I've missed you, Anna.'

She looked at him in surprise.

'Have you?'

'I can't bear not being with you. I still love you so much.'

His fingers gripped her shoulders.

'But, after what you said at Laura's funeral, all your doubts . . . you don't trust me, do you, Anna? You think those fires . . .'

Anna buried her face in his shirt.

'I need to be sure, Cameron, that's all.'

He held her at arms' length, his eyes full of sadness, and then he moved away, striding across the beach to where Sally was sitting, talking to some of her friends.

The day was a great success, and when everyone had gone, except Cameron, they sat down together.

'I've had such a lovely day, darling, Anna. Thank you. We'll do the same on my ninetieth.'

'Of course we will, Gran,' Anna said, hugging her. 'You will stay over, won't you, Cameron? It's such a long time since we've seen you. And I'm sure you and Anna have a lot to catch up with. Answer that phone, dear, will you? I'm really too exhausted to make the effort.'

Anna went into the hall. Probably another wellwisher for Gran. But it, wasn't!

Anna's hand trembled as she listened to the voice at the end of the phone.

'Cameron!' she called after only moments. 'It's the foreman working over at Trevellion Farm. Thought you were still away, so thought he'd better let me know. There's a fire!'

Cameron leaped to his feet and headed for the door, with Anna hot on his heels, calling to Sally to stay put. They would keep her informed as to what had happened.

Anna soon guessed Cameron must be breaking the speed limit as the car raced down the lanes, swinging round bends. They could see black smoke curl upwards long before they reached the rutted track leading to the farm. Flames blazed high into the air from the roof and flickered through every window of one wing of the house.

'Oh, Cameron!' she called out as they leaped from the car.

Tears blurred Anna's eyes as she looked at his taut face and felt his fingers twist into her palm. They stood, too horrified to move, spray from cascades of water settling on their skin.

After an hour or more one of the firemen came over.

'We've got it well under control now, sir. It's just that one wing. Was work being carried out there?'

'No,' Cameron replied. 'No. We've yet to begin on that part. Do you know how it started?'

The fireman nodded.

'Arson. Bit of luck your foreman was around. Called us as soon as he saw it. Place wouldn't have stood a chance otherwise.'

Cameron turned his head, eyes searching.

'Where is he? I must thank him.'

118

'Went in the ambulance with the other chap over to Truro.'

'Other chap? One of the other workmen?'

'Dunno, sir. Pretty bad way he was in, though.'

CHAPTER TWELVE

A nurse led them to a room off the main ward. The man sitting on a chair outside looked startled when he saw Cameron. Puzzled, he turned his head towards the room behind him, and then back again.

'Cameron! But I thought it was you over at Trevellion. I'd never have let him in otherwise.'

'Calm down, Jim. Let's take this slowly. What are you talking about?'

'Him as started the fire. Spitting image of you. Said he'd brought a can of stuff to clean that fireplace.'

He ran grimy fingers through his grey hair.

'I was so sure it was you, Cameron. He went on up the stairs. Then I caught a whiff of something. Petrol!'

His expression twisted as he continued.

'I ran straight up there after him, and found him striking a match when I came in the door. Must've made him jump and he spilled some petrol on his clothes.'

His hands knotted into each other.

'It was horrible, Cameron. Horrible, and nothing I could do to stop it. Went up like a bonfire. Nothing I could do.'

The man's shoulders began to shake as he wept.

'No-one could have done anything, Jim. No-one.'

Cameron swung round to the nurse.

'Can we see . . .'

'I'm afraid not.'

She lowered her head.

'He's very badly burned.'

'But he's my brother!' Cameron roared.

'Your brother? Well, in that case . . .'

She hesitated for a moment, eyeing him warily.

'You must be prepared . . .'

Cameron pushed open the door and Anna followed, closing her eyes when she saw the swathed figure on the bed. Only a blackened mouth was visible through the layers of gauze.

'Ryan. Oh, Ryan!'

Cameron's voice broke, and through her own tears, Anna watched the charred lips curve into Ryan's final smile . . .

'Never let his brother have anything he wanted himself, did Ryan,' Sally murmured sadly, stroking Anna's hair, as they sat together on the sofa later that night. 'Even as a child, and Cameron usually gave way.'

'Except over Trevellion Farm,' Anna said.

'And you, darling.'

Anna lifted her head.

'Me? Ryan hated me, Gran.'

Sally smiled.

'Maybe, but his brother loved you and was going to marry you. Ryan couldn't allow that.

121

Cameron must never win.'

'But in the end I have.'

They both looked up, surprised to see Cameron standing in the doorway.

'I thought you were still over at Trevellion,' Sally said.

'Nothing more I can do there. Once it's daylight it'll be easier to assess the damage.'

'Well, I'm off to bed. Now I'm eighty, I've a good excuse. Good-night, my darlings.'

Anna snuggled into the crook of Cameron's arm.

'I'm so sorry about what happened, and that I doubted you.'

He kissed the top of her head.

'It's the end of a chapter, Anna. Without Ryan, nothing can ever be the same again. His jealousy and greed have caused so much disaster, though, what with Grandpa and Laura and all his other tricks and ploys. But, in spite of that, we're still together, and always will be, won't we?'

'Always,' she whispered. 'Life is a series of changes, some good, some bad. It can never be otherwise.'

She raised her face to his and kissed him.

'But my love for you will never change, Cameron.'

'Nor mine for you,' he whispered.